The Mystery Writers of America Award for out-
standing achievement in mystery, crime and sus-
pense fiction has become the highest honor accord-
ed to authors in this field. That the MWA Award
for The Best Mystery Novel was won by Charlotte
Armstrong for her thriller A DRAM OF POISON
came as no surprise to her fans—or to the re-
viewers.

"A real spellbinder."

CLARK KINNAIRD, PARADE OF BOOKS

*"A brilliant psychological terror story . . . honed to
razor edge."*

OAKLAND TRIBUNE

*". . . a thriller of first rank . . . not without psy-
chological validity . . . a vivid portrayal of possibil-
ities."*

PSYCHIATRIC QUARTERLY

*". . . gathers speed and tension as it grows . . .
mounting desperation . . . developed with humor,
pathos and excitement."*

PITTSBURGH PRESS

A
Dram
of
Poison

BY CHARLOTTE ARMSTRONG

A FAWCETT CREST BOOK

FAWCETT PUBLICATIONS, INC., GREENWICH, CONN.
MEMBER OF AMERICAN BOOK PUBLISHERS COUNCIL, INC.

A Fawcett Crest Book reprinted by arrangement with
Coward-McCann, Inc. This book contains the complete text
of the original hardcover edition.

Seventh Fawcett Crest Printing, March 1970

Published by Fawcett World Library
67 West 44th Street, New York, N. Y. 10036
Printed in the United States of America

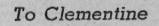

To Clementine

Chapter I

THE TALL MAN switched on the light. "I won't be a minute," he said.

The shorter man looked around the room, which was a laboratory. He ambled over to gaze, without understanding, at some apparatus.

"It's here somewhere," said Paul Townsend, lifting and shifting papers on the desk, opening the left top drawer. "Letter I meant to mail. Simply forgot. Now where . . . ?" He was an extremely good looking man, six feet high, in prime state at thirty-seven. His handsome face wore a little fussy frown.

"Take your time," said Mr. Gibson, who was older, in no hurry whatever, and who liked to browse. "What's all this?"

"Ah . . ." Paul Townsend found the letter. "Got it. That? That's poison."

"What have you done? Made a collection?" Mr. Gibson peered at a double rank of little square-bottomed bottles aligned to the fraction of an inch, neatly labeled, behind the glass doors of a cupboard.

"Lot of the stuff we use seems to be poisonous," Paul Townsend told him. "So best it's locked up." He came, dangling his letter between two fingers, and peered, too. "Sure is quite a collection," he said innocently.

"Looks like some gourmet's spice cupboard," said Mr. Gibson admiringly. "What are these good for?"

"Different things."

"I never heard of ninety per cent of them."

"Well . . ." said Paul Townsend in a forgiving way.

"Death and destruction," murmured Mr. Gibson, "in small packages." He put his forefinger on the glass door. (He fleetingly remembered having once been a little boy pushing his finger, just so, against the glass of a candy counter.) "Which would you advise?"

"What?" said Townsend, batting his long eyelashes.

Mr. Gibson smiled; delicate lines spread from his eye-corners like tiny peacocks' tails. "I'm taking a poetical view," he said whimsically, "of two dozen bottles of death. I don't think the way you do. Can't help it. Teach poetry, you know." He mocked himself good-humoredly and declaimed, "To cease upon the midnight with no pain . . ."

"Oh," said Townsend a little stupidly. "Well, if you mean what will knock you out quick and easy, take that one."

"That one?" Mr. Gibson made no sense of the poly-syllabic word on the label to which his host now pointed. He couldn't think how it could possibly be pronounced by a human tongue. The number on the label was 333, which was simple and stuck in the brain. "What will it do?"

"Just kill you," said Paul Townsend. "No taste. No smell."

"No color," murmured the other.

"No pain."

"How do you know that?" Mr. Gibson had fine gray eyes and they were lit with intelligent curiosity.

Townsend blinked again. "Know what?"

"That there is no pain? Or no taste, for that matter? Fella's knocked out, as you say. You can't ask him, can you?"

"Well, I . . . understand there's just no time for pain," said Townsend a little uncomfortably. "Ready?"

"Quite a place," said Mr. Gibson, giving a last look around.

Townsend had his finger on the light switch. "Wait a minute . . ." He frowned. He was like a housewife with unexpected company. He saw deficiencies in his house-keeping. "I see something should have been put away Maybe *it* wouldn't kill you, but . . . Now who left that out, I wonder? Would you mind turning away for a second?"

"Turning? Oh. Not at all." Mr. Gibson obligingly

turned his back and stared at a cupboard full of breakers
and tubes on the opposite wall. It's glass door made quite
an efficient mirror, if you selected with your mind only the
reflections, out of all you were seeing with your eyes. So
Mr. Gibson idly watched Paul Townsend take a small tin
of something from a table top, produce a key from a
hiding place, put the tin inside the poison cupboard, re-
lock the door, rehide the key. "O.K.," said Townsend.
"Sorry, but I like to be absolutely careful."

Mr. Gibson said, "Of course," softly. It didn't occur to
him to confess to his acquaintance that he now had a
very good idea where the key was kept. This Townsend
was a friendly chap who had happened to be eating a
meal in the same off-campus restaurant and who had
offered Mr. Gibson a ride home on this chilly January
evening. No need to explain to the man. Mr. Gibson
hated to embarrass him. And surely it did not matter.

He began to muse, instead, on poison. Why were there
substances created of which men must not eat? Fire, water,
air . . . all good for man . . . could yet, in quantity, in
excess, or out of place, destroy him. Was it possible that
poisons, too, had all their measures? Were they, in proper
quantity, or place, or time, good, too? In minute quantity
perhaps? Was it a question of discovering how much, or
where, or when?

"What's that number Three Thirty-three *good* for?" he
asked as they left the building.

"Nobody knows yet," Townsend said amiably. "But it
wouldn't be a bad way to die."

Mr. Gibson had no wish for death. He forgot about it
and looked up at the moon. "It is a beauteous evening,
calm and free . . ." he murmured.

"Nice night," agreed Townsend. "Little chilly, though.
I'll drop you off now. Thanks for waiting. Then I'll get
along home."

"Don't forget to mail your letter," said Mr. Gibson in
friendly prose. "There's a box on my corner."

It was Mr. Gibson's birthday. Characteristically, he
hadn't mentioned it. He was fifty-five years old.

He made his thanks and his good night and walked up
one flight to his big and only room. He lit the lamp, took
off his shoes, placed tobacco handy, selected his book. He
was a bachelor.

It was quiet there. It was cozy in a masculine way. It was a little backwater and in it Kenneth Gibson was content. To himself, it seemed that his life had been spent in a series of little backwaters. He had never breasted the full turbulence of the center currents, but like a gentle, unresisting leaf had slipped along the edges of the stream, been caught and held in this or that small stopping place, slipped out, only to be carried into another and yet another, until he had sailed finally into this particular quiet reach where there was no storm but only the gentlest of ripples from time to time.

He had his niche of usefulness. He liked his work and liked his life. He had a feeling that it was soon over. If another ten or twenty years went by softly in the same pattern it would not seem long. He wasn't an aggressive or an ambition-pressured man.

Four weeks after his fifty-fifth birthday, Mr. Gibson went to a funeral. There he met a young woman named Rosemary James.

It was old Professor James who had given up the ghost. The college rallied to its own. He had been retired for some eight years, had fallen, indeed, into irascible irrationality. But he had once been the college's own and so he must have a well-patronized funeral. The word was given.

Other faculty members met his only daughter, Rosemary, for the first time that day. But Kenneth Gibson met her most significantly because of a quality he had that he, himself, thought of as a weakness. He had the gift, or the burden, of empathy.

To himself, it was a weak sensitivity. Oh, he had learned, in fifty-five years, to manage it pretty well. It had hurt him very much during the First World War.

Having been born in the first month of a new century he was, of course, eighteen years old in 1918. He had grown up in a very small town in Indiana, a backwater, with a father who owned a hardware store and was a cheerful tactless man, and a mother named Maureen (Grady) who was a little woman with a fanciful mind. He had gone from the village high school directly to the war, because it had seemed the fervently "right" thing to do at the time.

Young, compact of body and muscle, spruce and neat —for Kenneth Gibson from the beginning was one of those people who always look washed and orderly by some natural gift—even then, he had evidently had an affinity for paper and ink. He went through the war, in the fierce breeches and puttees of the day, as a clerk. Cheerful, willing, and meticulous, he had made a good one. But, although he marked paper with ink in some not unperilous places, he never actually got into a battle. So, when it was all over, nobody knew nor was anyone told that this lad was numb with horror. Nobody ever knew how his essentially fastidious soul had been lacerated by the secrets of slaughter he had come to know and had had to bear. Nobody, in those days, would have conceded the wounds in his mind to be either plausible or important. There were too many horrors experienced. He had only been able to imagine them.

Saying nothing, he dived for sanctuary and healing into books. He went to college. He escaped flaming with the youth of that time because he was older than, and a little out of step with, his classmates. Besides, he was busy healing his invisible wounds in his own way.

His father died the year he got his Master's. His mother was left in straitened circumstances, so Kenneth helped support her in her own place. He did not transport her, for he knew this would not be kind. But he took the burden. It never occurred to him, while he worked at his first meagerly paid teaching job, sent money to his mother, and even helped his younger sister Ethel on her way through college at the same time, that all this was any sacrifice. It simply seemed that his own life, as he saw it, had hit one of those backwaters. To clerk through the war was such, surely. To be a young teacher with family responsibilities was only another. He hewed to the line. He had to. No giddy young days for him.

In 1932 his mother, after an expensive illness, died, and he mourned her, but the depression was on the land and whoever had forborne to fire him from his job while his mother was alive, forbore no longer.

Ethel, eight years his junior, was out of school by this time, of course, and she was earning, and she helped him, for she too had a sense of responsibility and was reliable. He was deep in debt while he scrambled for odd jobs during those bad times.

When, at last, he got another modest teaching job he went into this backwater thankfully. It was a long grind to work off his debts, lean quiet years. But he did it. He learned to take a good deal of pleasure in seeing the old obligations melt slowly away as he satisfied them. When at last he was free and moderately prospering, the world was into the tense months after Munich.

He was thirty-seven by now, a bachelor. Of *course* a bachelor. He had never had enough to offer a woman of his own. Security. Prestige. Whatever. Before he got around to risking any personal alliance came 1941, and he went to war the second time.

Naturally, he clerked. Well-seasoned, perfectly at home with paper, he spent the war years in an office in a backwater—bearing this and indeed glad of it—for his soul could still wince. But never quite understanding what he was doing there that mattered at all. He only knew that somebody thought it was his duty, which he, of course, did.

In 1945 he emerged from this and met his sister Ethel in New York and said goodbye. Ethel, his only kin, had never married either. (Was it something about the mother and father?) She was a grown woman—getting along herself, in fact—thirty-seven years old. Never a beauty, Ethel, but clever and industrious, and well established in a good job. Ethel did not need him. In fact, she frightened him a little, at that time, by her ease in the turbulent business world, her blunt courage, her perfect independence.

He admired her for it very much. But he said an affectionate, but not woeful, goodbye and came to California to a job in the English Department of a small liberal arts college in a little city that sprawled and spilled over a sunny valley. His permanent backwater.

Here, for ten years, without even a glimpse of his only kin, he taught about poetry—to football players, coeds, and all variety of young people—by a kind of moral supremacy. Kenneth Gibson was obviously no Bohemian wretch with wild eyes and rebellious ideas and, equally obviously, no silken aesthete looking down a haughty nose upon the bourgeoisie. He was, rather obviously, a nice decent well-contained little man, five feet eight, still taut and compact, by no means showing his age, although his fair hair had inconspicuous threads of white in it—a most respectable man, with fine gray eyes, with a nice mouth that often wore a touch of humor on it.

The young were rocked by the fact that *this* man

actually took this stuff seriously. It behooved them to look into it themselves and see what it was worth, then.

So he did his work well, quite often succeeding in communicating his own conviction that poetry was not necessarily sissy . . . which was an achievement greater than he realized, poetry having the repute it has today.

He had his books, his acquaintances, his solitude, his work, his cozy room, and the beauty of trees, the magnificence of sky, the lift of the mountains on the horizon, and the music of men's ancient thoughts, to sustain his spirit. He had his life and he thought he foresaw how it would end. But then he met Rosemary James at her father's funeral.

Chapter II

MR. GIBSON sat decorously with his colleagues in the gloomy little chapel and endured the cruel, but necessary, ceremony by a little trick he had of deliberately disengaging a lot of his attention. When it was over he realized, with a pang of outrage, that off at the side, behind the curtain in the "family room," Rosemary James had been sitting through it all alone. If he had known! He had never met the girl—poor thing—but if he had known, he would have churned up the community to find somebody —anybody—to be with her. Or he would have sat in there *himself*. He hated a funeral—anybody's funeral—and he found himself imagining her ordeal, and furious that it had *been*.

When he took her hand, beside the grave, he felt the vibration of her lonely anguish. He knew in the marrow of his bones that she was exhausted and in despair and had to have hope. Had to have something, however trival, ahead of her. She could die without it.

So standing in the sunshine, on the sad turf, with the flowers heaped behind them, he said to her, "Your father must have many papers. I wonder if any of them should be published."

"I don't know," said Rosemary.

"I wonder," said Mr. Gibson. "Would you like me to go through them for you? We can't tell. There may be valuable things."

"Oh," she said, "I suppose there might. I wouldn't know." She seemed timid, poor thing.

"I'd be very glad to help if I can," he said gently.

"Thank you, Mr.—Gibson?"

"Then may I come over . . . perhaps tomorrow?"

"Please do," she said tremulously. "It's very good of you. Won't it be a trouble?"

"It will be a pleasure," he said. The word was deliberate. To speak of pleasure at the graveside was rough, was shocking. But she needed to have inserted into her imagination such a word.

She thanked him once more, stumblingly. A shy young woman, too upset, too bewildered, to have any poise. Not a child, of course. In her late twenties probably. Slim . . . in fact a pitifully thin body, trembling now with strain and fatigue but standing up to it somehow. A white face. Frightened blue eyes, with little folds of skin at the upper outer edges that came down sadly. A lined white brow. Limp, lifeless brown hair. An unpainted mouth, pathetically trying to smile and yet not smile. Well, she could look forward now, if ever so little, to tomorrow.

"We'll see," said Mr. Gibson, and _he_ smiled in full. "Who can tell?" he added cheerfully. "We might find some treasure."

Her eyes changed shape and he saw the flicker of wonder, of hope, and he was quite pleased with himself.

On his way home, he fumed. Poor thing! Looked as if a vampire bat had been drinking her blood. And perhaps he had. The arrogant angry old man whose brain had betrayed him and who lived out his final decade flubbing about helplessly hunting his own thoughts, which kept eluding him. Mr. Gibson was so very sorry for the girl. Poor, unattractive, tired, beaten creature—terrible ordeal shouldn't have _been_ there all alone!

The Jameses lived on the first floor of an old house near the campus. The moment Mr. Gibson entered the hall, he received the news of poverty and decay and a sense of darkness. If this place had ever had any colors, they had now all faded down into a uniform muddiness that defeated light. Everything, although quite clean, was somehow stained. Everything was old. And there was a clutter that comes of never having guests and therefore never seeing one's home with a fresh eye.

Nevertheless, he perceived that Rosemary had smoothed her dull hair carefully, that her dress was fresh from the ironing board, and that she had a string of blue beads on. It was typical of Mr. Gibson that these observations did not make him want to smile. They made him want to weep.

She greeted him timidly and seriously. She took him with nervous dispatch directly to the old man's lair.

"Well," he said in flat astonishment.

The old flat-topped desk was heaped with pieces of paper, lying at mad angles to one another.

"It looks like a haystack," said Rosemary with a spirited aptness that surprised him.

"Sure does." He appreciated her phrase. Smiled over it. "And it's our job to find the needle. Now come, you sit here. We'll start in the middle of the top and dig our way straight down to the bare wood. O.K. with you?"

They sat down. Mr. Gibson began to spin out of his own substance an atmosphere of cheerful, purposeful, organized endeavor. Soon she was breathing less shallowly and her lips were parted. She was intelligent.

But after a while absolutely nothing could save the situation from tragedy but a sense of humor. The old professor had scratched on paper during many hours. But his handwriting was atrocious, and worse, what he had written, where it was decipherable, seemed to have no reasonable meaning.

Mr. Gibson, in automatic defense, began to force himself to see the funny side. "If that is a capital T, as it may be for all I know," said he in semicomical despair, "then the word can be 'Therefore.' What do you think? Of course, it might just as well be 'Somewhere.'"

"Or 'However'?" said Rosemary earnestly.

"'However' is a distinct runner-up," he drawled. "Or even 'Whomever.'"

"'Whatever'?"

"I have a psychic feeling there's an 'f' in it. How about 'Wherefore'? 'Wherefore art thou Romeo?' D'you know, Miss James, the word might even be 'Romeo'." It was heavy work to be light about this.

"Oh, I don't think so," she said seriously. And then she looked startled. Then she giggled.

It was as if a phoenix had risen from some ashes. Her giggle was rather low-pitched and melodious. The tiny folds at the upper-outer corners of her eyes were built for laughter. It was their function. They were droll. The eyes themselves lost their dusty look and became a little shiny. Even her skin seemed to gain a tinge of color.

"I'll betcha we could make it read anything we like," said Mr. Gibson enthusiastically. "Do you know anything about the Bacon-Shakespeare ciphers?" She didn't. She listened while he told her some of the wild aspects of that affair.

After that, while she was still relaxed and amused, he said gently, "You know, I think we had best look at the bottom of the pile."

"Earlier, you mean?" She *was* intelligent.

"I think so, my dear."

"He . . . tried so hard." Her handkerchief came up.

"It was brave to keep trying," he said. "It really was. And we'll keep trying, too."

"There are mounds—" she said bravely, "of papers in the drawers. Some typewritten . . ."

"Hurray."

"But Mr. Gibson, it will take so much time . . ."

"Of course," he said gently. "I never expected to go through it all in an hour. Did you?"

"You mustn't get tired."

"Are you tired?" He thought she was.

"I wondered . . . Do you drink tea?"

"When I am offered any," he said.

She rose awkwardly and went to fetch the tea which had been her own bold idea. Mr. Gibson waited by himself staring soberly at the desk and all this waste of paper. He didn't think they were going to find any treasure. Also, he knew that he had, once again, been foolish and rash. He'd let an impulse lead him. When would he learn not to do these things? He had given hope where there was not much real chance. He had best softly kill the hope he'd raised. But he feared very much that it was too important to her.

While they drank tea and ate some thin store cookies . . . a tiny feast she'd made as dainty as she could . . . Mr. Gibson felt that he must pry.

"Do you own this house?" he asked her.

"Oh, no. We only rented this half."

"Will you stay on here?"

"I can't. It's too big. Too much for me."

He feared she meant too expensive. "Forgive me for asking, but is there money? Funds of any kind?"

"I can sell the furniture. And the car."

"Ah, a car?"

"It's ten years old." He saw that she swallowed. "But it must be worth something."

"Your father's income was . . . for his lifetime?"

"Yes."

"There is *nothing?*" he guessed sharply.

"Well . . . the furniture . . ." She stopped pretending that the furniture was of any value and met his eyes. "I will just have to get a job. I don't know just what . . ." She twisted the beads. "I hoped . . ." Her eyes went to the papers.

"Can you type?" he asked quickly. She shook her head. "Have you ever held a job, Miss James?"

"No, I . . . Dad needed me. When Mama died I was the only one left, you see."

It was easy for Mr. Gibson to understand perfectly what had happened to her. "Have you anyone who can advise you?" he asked. "Relatives?"

"Nobody."

"How old are you?" he asked her gently "Since I am old enough to be your father, you mustn't mind if I ask these things."

"I am thirty-two. And it's late, isn't it? But I'll find something to do."

He thought she needed somewhere to rest, above everything. "Have you a friend? Is there some place you could go?"

"I'll have to find a place to live," she said evasively. He divined that there was no such friend. The difficult old man no doubt had driven all well-meaning people away. "The landlord wants me to be gone by the first of March," Rosemary said. "He wants to redecorate. It certainly needs it." She made a nervous grimace.

Mr. Gibson cursed the landlord silently. "You're in a predicament, aren't you?" he remarked cheerfully. "Let me snoop around and see what kinds of jobs there are. May I?"

Her eyes widened again. The flesh lifted. The look was wonder. She said, "I don't want to be any trouble . . ."

"That wouldn't be any trouble," he said gently. "I can send out feelers, you know. Perhaps easier than you could. 'Wanted: well-paying job for person with no business experience whatsoever.' Look here, my dear, it's not impossible! After all, babies are born and *they've* had no business experience and yet they eventually do get jobs." He'd coaxed a smile out of her. "Now, we may find something here, but I had better say this, Miss James. It is neither easy nor is it a quick thing to find a publisher. It's very slow, I'm afraid. Nor is there very much money for academic kinds of writing."

"Thank you so much for being so kind, Mr. Gibson. But you don't have to be."

She wasn't rejecting him. In the droop of her body was all her weakness and fatigue. But she was, nevertheless, sitting as straight as she *could*, and looking as competent as was possible. She was trying to free him.

But what she had just said was not true, alas. He did have to be kind. He did have to try to help her . . . and keep her going with tidbits of hope. He couldn't imagine how to do otherwise.

He said easily, "I'll tell you what. Suppose I come again . . . let's see . . . on Friday afternoon? We'll attack the typewritten stuff. Now don't you disturb it. Meantime, I'll snoop. And I did enjoy the tea," he told her.

She did not thank him all over again, for which he was grateful as he got out into the living air.

Mr. Gibson was troubled all during Thursday because he knew he was being weak and wouldn't let himself think about it.

When he went again on Friday (He had to! He'd promised) the typewritten pages in the professor's lower desk drawers turned out to be, for the most part, correspondence which on the professor's side became progressively more angry and less coherent as the nerve paths in his brain had begun to tangle and cross one another. Mr. Gibson pretended it was very interesting. It was. But as tragedy. Not treasure.

Nevertheless, Mr. Gibson strung out the task and kept calling. Oh, he knew exactly what he was doing. When he thought about it he did not approve at all. It was weak. He had entangled himself, and every visit wove another strand into the web. And he knew better. Nobody knew better than he that he ought to withdraw gracefully. She was no burden of his.

He could withdraw. In modern days, in the United States of America, no corpse lies on the street slain by destitution. There were charities and public institutions. There was social succor. Nor would Rosemary blame him if he slipped out of her affairs. She would only continue to be grateful for all he had done or tried to do so far.

But he was incapable of this kind of common sense. By now, he knew exactly how to make her smile. No organized charity could know *this*. It was a little ridiculous how much this weighed with him. As he knew. But he'd just gotten into the whole business too far. He had seen himself do it, but he had looked away. So had Rosemary seen it. She had even warned him. But now it was too late. He had constituted himself as the holder of the carrot of hope before this donkey's nose . . . without which she might stop, cease, or even die. . . .

Meantime, dealers came to look at the furniture and offer contemptuous minimums. The books were worth pitifully little in cash. One day a man said he'd give fifty dollars for the ancient car. By the time Rosemary conferred with Mr. Gibson and decided to accept it, he had withdrawn even this offer. Her possessions were without value.

Meantime, also, Mr. Gibson snooped for jobs in Rosemary's behalf. He discovered that there were indeed some which did not demand experience. They definitely required good health and some strength, instead. Rosemary did not have these qualifications, either. On the contrary, it was evident to Mr. Gibson that she was heading for a serious breakdown. He was able to see her rooms become even more neglected because she could do nothing about it. He guessed that she was able to keep her person neat only by a terrible effort, by a stubborn flickering of innate pride. Otherwise, she was limp with the inertia of physical and emotional exhaustion. And to call, to talk, to coax a little ease into her face, three times a week, this—although vital—was not really enough.

What was she to do? This began to obsess him. She had no funds, no strength. She seemed to eat . . . he wasn't sure how well. She'd have no place to eat, or sleep, soon, for the 1st of March loomed closer.

On the 25th of February he marched in and announced peremptorily that he had just paid the rent here for April. "You need the time. You *must* have it. All right. You owe me the money. That's nothing. I have owed money . . ."

She broke and cried until he was alarmed.

"Now, mouse," he said. "Please . . ." His throat ached with hers.

So she told him she was afraid her mind was going, as her father's had gone, because she was so weighted by a numbness and a languor. He, appalled, insisted upon bringing his own doctor to take a look at her.

The doctor scoffed. Old Professor James' trouble was not inheritable. This woman was frighteningly run-down. Underweight. Malnourished. Anemic. Nervously exhausted. *He* knew what she needed. Medicine, diet, and a long rest. He seemed to think he had solved everything.

Mr. Gibson chewed his lips.

"Say, where do you come in, Gibson?" the doctor asked amiably. "In loco parentis?"

Mr. Gibson said he guessed *so*. He bought the medcines. He gave her orders. He knew that this was not enough.

The same evening, one of his colleagues, casually encountered, nudged his ribs and said, "You're a sly one, Gibson. I hear you're shining up to old James' daughter these days. When's the wedding, hm?"

Chapter III

O<small>N THE IDES</small> of April, in the afternoon (for he always came after classes, by daylight), Rosemary was sitting in a mud-colored old armchair in her living room. Mr. Gibson could remark the fluff of dust accumulating along its seams. He thought to himself, It is impossible for anyone to be healthy in this dreadful place. I have got to get her out of here.

She had her hair pulled back today and tied in a hank at the back of her neck with a faded red ribbon. This did not make her look girlish. She looked haggard.

She said, as primly as if she'd memorized it, "I feel so much better. The medicine is doing me good, I'm sure. And to know what the trouble is, that's been comforting." She dragged her eyelids up. "Mr. Gibson, I want you to go away . . . not come any more."

"Why?" he said with a pang.

"Because I am nobody of yours. You shouldn't worry about me. You weren't even a friend of ours."

Mr. Gibson did not misunderstand. "Surely, I am a friend now," he chided gently.

"You are," she admitted with a dry gasp, "and the only one. . . . But you *have* helped me. It is enough. Congratulate yourself. Please."

He got up and walked about. He admired her spunk. He approved of it. But he felt upset. "What will you do on the first of May?"

"If nothing else . . . I'll go to the county," she said.

"I see. You feel distressed about me? You don't want me to try to help you any more?"

She shook her head dumbly. She looked as if she had spent her very last ounce of energy.

"They tell me," mused Mr. Gibson aloud, looking at the horrible wallpaper, "that it is more blessed to give than to receive. But it does seem to me, in that case, *somebody* has to be willing to receive. And do it graciously," he added rather sternly. She winced as if he had slapped her. "Oh, I know it isn't easy," he assured her quickly.

Then he hesitated. But not for long.

The trouble was, his imagination had been working. He ought to have known that if a thing can be vividly imagined, it can be done. It probably will be done. He sat down and leaned forward earnestly.

"Rosemary, suppose there was something you could do for me?"

"Anything I could ever do for you," she choked, "I'd be bound to do."

"Good. Now let's take it for granted, shall we, that you are grateful and stop repeating that? It's a terrible bore for both of us. And I do not enjoy seeing you cry, you know. I don't enjoy it at all."

She squeezed her lids together.

"I am fifty-five years old," he said. Her damp lids opened in surprise. "I don't look it?" He smiled. "Well, as I always say, I've been pickled in poetry. I earn seven thousand a year. I wanted you to know these . . . er . . . statistics before I asked you to marry me."

She clapped both hands over her face and eyes.

"Listen a minute," he went on gently. "I've never married. I've never had a home made for me by a woman. Perhaps I have been missing something . . . in that alone. Now there's a skill you have, Rosemary. You know how to keep a house. You've done it for years. You can do it, and very nicely, I'm sure, once you feel strong again. So I was thinking . . ."

She did not move nor even look between her fingers.

"It might be a good bargain between us," he went on. "We *are* friends, whatever you say. I think we are not incompatible. We've had some pleasant hours, even in all this difficulty. We might make good companions. Can you look at it as if it were to be an experiment? A venture? Let us not say its forever. Suppose we found we didn't enjoy being together? Why, in these days, you know, divorce is quite acceptable. Especially . . . Rosemary, are you a religious woman?"

"I don't know," she said pitifully behind her hands.

"Well, I thought," he continued, "if instead of a holy pledge . . . we made a bargain . . ." He began to speak louder. "My dear, I am not in love with you," he stated bluntly. "I don't speak of love or romance. At my age, it would be a little silly. I neither expect romantic love nor intend to give it. I am thinking of an arrangement. I am trying to be frank. Will you let me know if you understand me?"

"I do," she said brokenly. "I understand what you mean. But it's no real bargain at all, Mr. Gibson. I am no use to anybody . . ."

"No, you are not, not at the moment," he agreed cheerfully. "I wouldn't expect you to do the wash next Monday, you know. But I am thinking, and please think seriously too. . . . Although there is one point I'd like to make quickly. I don't want to cheat you."

"Cheat me?" she said hoarsely.

"You are only thirty-two. Be frank with me."

She took her hands down. "How can I say I'd rather go on the county?" she said with sudden asperity.

"You could say it if it is so," he told her grinning. The

air in the room lightened. Everything seemed gayer. "Did you ever have a hobby, Rosemary?" he asked her.

"A hobby? Yes, I . . . once or twice. I had a garden. For a while I . . . liked to try to paint." She looked dazed.

"Let me confess, then. I am presently enchanted by the idea of making you well again. Of getting you up, Rosemary, and yourself, again. As a matter of fact, it is exactly as if to do so was a hobby of mine. Now then. Now, *that's* honest." He settled back. "How I'd like to!" he said wistfully. "I really would. I'd like to put you in a bright pleasant place and feed you up and see you get fat and sassy. I can't think," he sighed, "of anything that would be more fun."

She put her hands over her face and rocked her body.

"No?" he said quietly. "If the idea repels you, why of course it's not feasible. But what will you do, Rosemary? What will become of you? Don't you see that I can't stop worrying? How can you stop me if I can't stop myself? I wish you would let me lend you money, at least." He fidgeted.

"I can cook, Mr. Gibson," she said in a low voice.

He said in a moment, "Then, I'm afraid you will have to begin to call me Kenneth."

She said, "Yes, Kenneth, I will."

They were married on the 20th of April by a justice of the peace.

One of the witnesses was Paul Townsend.

This came about because, in the five-day flurry and excitement, when Mr. Gibson was house-hunting as hard as he could, he bumped into Paul Townsend, confided his problem, and Paul solved it.

"Say!" His handsome genial face lit up. "I've got just the place for you! It'd be perfect! My tenant left a week ago. The painters will be gone tomorrow What a coincidence! Gibson, you're *in!*"

"Where am I in?"

"In my cottage on the lot adjoining my own place. A regular honeymoon cottage."

"Furnished?"

"Of course, furnished. It's a little far out."

"How far?"

"Thirty minutes on the bus. You don't drive a car?"

"Rosemary has a car of sorts. An old monster. Not even worth selling."

"Well, then! There's a garage for it. How does this sound? Living room, bedroom, bath, big den—lots of bookshelves in there—dinette, kitchen. There's a fireplace . . ."

"Bookshelves?" said Mr. Gibson. "Fireplace?"

"And a garden."

"Garden?" said Mr. Gibson in a trance.

"I'm a nut on gardening myself. You come and see." Mr. Gibson went and saw, and succumbed.

The wedding took place at three in the afternoon in a drab office with no fanfar and not much odor of sanctity. The justice was a mat r-of-fact type who mumbled drearily. No one was pres nt except the necessary witnesses. Mr. Gibson had thought it best to ask none of his colleagues to watch him being married, in this manner, to this white-faced woman in her old blue suit who could scarcely stand up, whose gaunt finger shook so that he could scarcely force the ring over the knucklebone.

Then of course Rosemary had no people. And Mr. Gibson's only sister Ethel, although asked, for auld lang syne, could not come. She wrote that she supposed he would know what he was doing at his age, and she was happy for him if he was happy—that she would try to come to visit one day, perhaps during the summer, and then meet the bride. To whom she sent love.

It was an ugly dreary wedding. It made Mr. Gibson wince in his soul, but it was quick, soon over. He was able to take it as just necessary, like a disagreeable pill.

Chapter IV

PAUL TOWNSEND lived, together with his teenage daughter and his elderly mother-in-law, in a low stucco house of some size on a fair piece of land. Beside his driveway lay the driveway pertaining to the cottage. The cottage was built of brick and redwood and upon it vines really did grow. Mr. Gibson's books and papers (although still in boxes), and his neat day-bed, were already there in the large square shelf-lined room off the living room, and the lumbering old car that Professor James had bought years ago was already standing in the neat little garage when Mr. Gibson brought his bride home in a taxi. He opened the front door and led her in, making no attempt at the threshold gesture. He sat her down in a bright blue easy chair. She looked as if she were going to die.

But Mr. Gibson had his own ideas of healing and he plunged in, heart and soul. He had wangled a week away from his classes. He proposed to use it to settle. But the cottage had aroused in his own breast some instincts he'd never known about. He also proposed to make a home.

So, during that first hour, he bustled. He poured out his enthusiasms, all going forward. He made her look at color. Did she like the primrose yellow in the draperies? (He thought privately that the clean, fresh colors in this charming sun-drenched room would be health-giving in themselves.) Where would he put his record player? he wondered aloud, forcing her to consider the promise of music. Then he officiated in the kitchen. He was not a bad cook, himself, but he begged her advice. He did all he could to interest and tempt her.

Rosemary could not eat any supper. She was not ready for a future. She was collapsing after an escape from the past. There would be a hiatus. He feared she'd die of it.

So he insisted that she go at once to bed, in the soft-hued bedroom that would be hers alone. When he judged she was settled, he brought her the medicine. He touched the dry straw of her sad hair. He said, "Rest now." Her head turned weakly.

He spent the evening unpacking books and listening . . . sometimes toptoeing to her door to listen.

The next day she lay abed, unable to move, as good as dead. Only her eyes asked for mercy and patience.

Mr. Gibson had lots of patience. He was undaunted and took pains to make some very silly puns each time he brought her a snack to eat. He hooked up the record player and let music penetrate the whole little house. He believed in humor and in beauty and in color and in music and he mined the deepest faiths he had . . . for he *knew* he could heal her.

On the second morning, he went in to remove her breakfast tray and saw that she was lying against the pillow with her face turned to the window. Between the dainty white margins of the curtains there was visible a patch of ground planted with roses. On her face, for the first time in his knowledge of her, lay a look of peace.

"I used to love to sit on the ground with my hands in the dirt," she said to him. "There is something about earth on your hands . . ."

"Yes, there is. And something about light. And something about running water, too. Don't you think so?"

"Yes," she said stirring.

He thought this particular "yes" had a most positive sound to it. He went softly, however. He took care not to nag at her, not to bother.

On the third day Rosemary got up and dressed in a cotton frock. She began to make a brave effort to eat, as if she owed this to him. In the evening, he built a fire (for there is something about a fire, too) and he read to her. He read some poetry. It gave him such pleasure to realize that she was going to be the best pupil he had ever had. She listened so intently. It was lively to listen so. It was a spark of life which he would fan.

Once she said to him, during that evening, with a look of pain, "You are so sane." It made him wince to understand how eight years of her life had been spent alone with that which could not have been called sane. No wonder, he said to himself. No wonder it has nearly killed her.

Now his week off began to go leaping by. She helped dust some books. She couldn't, of course, dust many. Mr. Gibson had to go back to work on the Monday, so on Friday Mrs. Violette came in.

Mrs. Violette was produced for them by Paul Townsend. She was a cleaning woman; she worked for the Townsends in the afternoons. But she was a young person, very slim and quick, with shining black hair and skin of a soft peach color and a countenance of a smoothness and design that was foreign. At least there was something odd, and not plain American, about her looks—Near Eastern perhaps. One couldn't place her.

Mrs. Violette didn't concern herself with being placed. She was cool and detached, taciturn and competent. One knew that she could keep this little house clean with the back of one of her slim strong buff-colored hands. Mr. Gibson thought she would do admirably. She was not, thank heaven, some garrulous woe-loving old creature reduced to drudgery by adversities. She was fresh and self-respecting. She would be fine. Rosemary agreed, but wondered if it wouldn't cost too much.

"Until you are perfectly well," he told her, "Mrs. Violette is an economy. Now that's just sensible."

"At least *you* make it *sound* sensible," Rosemary said with a touch of life and opinion.

So Mr. Gibson went back to his classes on the Monday, convinced that Rosemary wasn't going to die.

He rode the buses. He wasn't much of a driver, for an automobile was a thing he had known, all his life, how to do without. So he left the ancient car in the garage until such time as Rosemary might wish to use it. She understood it, which was more than he did, and he rode his thirty minutes, brooding and half-smiling to himself over little schemes. For he was possessed by the joy of nurture which is closely akin, if not identical with, the deep joy of creation. He had never known this in his life before. It absolutely absorbed him.

Rosemary was eating well. She was stuffing herself to please him. (Ah, so it did!) When he came home, the little house would be shining from the administrations of Mrs. Violette, and Rosemary would recount to him how many eggs she'd had, how many glasses of milk, what toast. . . . And he'd say she'd be fat as a pig pretty soon and feel a sting behind his eyes.

One afternoon he came walking home, the two blocks from the bus stop, to see her sitting on the ground at the far side of the house, near the roses. He altered his course and stepped softly toward her on the grass. She looked up and her face was dirty where she had swiped an earthy hand across her nose. She was patting and combing the earth around one rose bush with her bare fingers.

This earth was dampish and richly dark. She told him it was in good tilth. Mr. Gibson squatted down to admire and, at the same time, to taste and turn and enjoy a word that was new to him. What a wonderful word! Tilth. He understood it immediately.

She said the roses needed mulchng and he learned about mulch. She showed him how delicately she had pruned this one rose bush, how the buds must be left to grow outward. She seemed to understand what the plant needed. It seemed to him that she felt toward this one

plant—all she could manage yet—much as he felt toward
her, Rosemary. He didn't say so. When he helped her to her
feet, it seemed to him that she sprang up rather lightly.
It made him happy.

Then one Saturday morning, puttering in his room,
he realized that, while he could hear Mrs. Violette in the
kitchen, he missed another presence in the house. He
looked out of all the windows and at last saw Rosemary
sitting in the back-yard grass, in the sun, with a hair-
brush in her hand. She was brushing her hair in slow
rhythm and while he watched she did not cease to brush
her hair. Something about the scene startled him. The
rhythm, the sensuous rhythm, the ritual of it, the strange-
ness . . . Rosemary was a woman. She was a mystery. One
day, when he had brought her to full life and health as
he would do, why, he did not know with whom he would
be living in this house! He did not know Rosemary, herself. . . .

Paul Townsend turned out to be an ideal landlord. He
was genial and easy, but he did not intrude. One day,
however, when three weeks had gone by and the Gibsons
could be presumed settled in, Paul invited them to supper.

It was their first social event.

Rosemary wore her best dress. Mr. Gibson admired
it aloud. It was a dullish blue, a pleasant enough dress.
But he fussed a little. As soon as ever she felt just like
it, he told her, she must buy at least two new dresses . . .
maybe three. Rosemary quietly promised that she would.
She accepted everything he urged upon her these days with
no more weak spilling of grateful tears. In fact, she was
full of grace in the matter of receiving.

They walked across the double driveway to Paul Townsend's house.

While not grand, this was certainly the home of a sol-
vent man. Paul Townsend, a chemical engineer, owned
the plant and laboratory down near the college, and it
must return him if not a fortune at least a pleasant living.

He was a widower. Mr. Gibson had never known his
wife, alive. Her picture was in this house many times.
It was a little sad to see how young the pictures were.
She did not look as if her daughter could be this tall
Jean, fifteen, and in high school. A pleasant child, with a
cropped and tousled dark head, fine white teeth in a
ready smile, excellent company manners. Then there was

Paul's mother-in-law, Mrs. Pyne, a cripple, poor soul, who inhabited a wheel chair.

Supper was not formal but nicely served and stiffly, politely eaten. Mr. Gibson watched Rosemary. Was she nervous about these people? Was it a strain? Was she strong enough?

The old lady asked kind commonplace questions, and told kind commonplace statistics about herself and the family. She had a thin, rather delicately boned face, and the tact not to mention her own disabilities. The young girl kept her place among her elders, served the meal, cleared the table afterward, and then excused herself to do her homework. Paul was a considerate host, full of good will and social anxiety.

But there are just so many commonplaces. Mr. Gibson set to work to dissolve the stiffness of this first meeting of Rosemary and her nearest neighbors. He was bound Rosemary was going to find it easy and pleasant to move into a world of friendly give and take. In fact, he talked a good deal for a while. At last, by prying and prodding for mutual interests, he discovered how to egg Paul on to talk about his garden. Rosemary began to listen and contribute. Mr. Gibson was eager to learn. Once Paul asked a silly punning question . . . whether Mr. Gibson had a sense of humus. Mr. Gibson was inspired to reply, "Not mulch." And Rosemary giggled. The old lady smiled indulgently and kept listening pleasantly as the session grew quite animated.

At ten o'clock they took their leave, for Mr. Gibson did not want Rosemary tired out. After the good nights and the kind parting phrases, they crossed the roofless porch at the front of Paul's house. They came down the five steps and crossed the double driveways in the soft chill air of night time. They went in at their own back door, skirting the shining new garbage cans, symbolic of a functioning house. They crossed the pale dim orderly kitchen and entered the living room, where a lamp had been left burning. The sense of home flowed into Mr. Gibson's heart.

"Wasn't that fun?" said he. "I thought *you* were having a good time."

Rosemary stood there, in the blue dress, slowly shrugging off the dark sweater from around her shoulders. She looked brooding and intense. "I have never known," she said vibrantly, "it was possible to have so good a time. I never, never, knew . . ."

It rather shocked him. He could think of nothing to reply. She tossed the sweater into her chair and sat down and looked up at him and smiled. "Read to me, Kenneth, please," she said coaxingly, "for just ten minutes? Until I simmer down?"

"If you drink your milk and eat your cookies."

"Yes, I will. Bring four."

So he fetched the nourishment. He opened a book. He read to her.

Afterward, she licked a cookie crumb from her forefinger. She thanked him with a drowsy smile. . . .

Kenneth Gibson went into his room, which had by now acquired the look of all the places he had ever lived for long, the mellow order, the masculine coziness. He went to bed a little bewildered. He was beginning not to understand her.

Chapter V

ON THE 19th of May, Rosemary got up before him to make his breakfast. She had on a new cotton frock, for "around the house," she said. It was pink and a particularly springlike pink, somehow. She chattered away. She would like to try feeding the border with a new kind of fertilizer. Paul Townsend said it did wonders. Did he think $3.95 was too much to spend on it? And would he like roast lamb for dinner? Did he prefer mint sauce or a sweet mint jelly with his lamb? Wasn't the early sun on the little stone wall a lovely sight! Pale gold on the gray. Why was sunlight, in the morning, so crisp—and then, by noon, more like cloudy honey?

"Shadows?" he speculated. "Some day you should try to paint what you see, Rosemary."

She wasn't good enough, she said, although to *try* . . . At least, she announced, tossing her head, Mrs. Violette must wash and starch the kitchen curtains. They'd be nicer crisp to match the mornings. Didn't he think so?

Mr. Gibson sat there at the table, watching her and

listening, and his eyes suddenly cleared. Scales fell. He saw Rosemary, not as she had been, or as he had been thinking of her, but as she *was,* this morning.

The crisp frock showed a figure that, while slim, certainly could not be called skinny any more. Neither was it bent and hollow with the posture of weakness. On the contrary, she sat quite upright and above her snug waist swelled a charming bosom, and the shoulder bones were covered with sweet flesh. Then her hair! Why, her hair was thick and shining and full of chestnut lights! Where had it come from? Whence *this* face? *This* face was not pasty white nor did the flesh droop in sad rumples. It was almost firm, and sun-gilded to a rosy-gold, and the lines in her forehead were a maturity (more interesting than the bare bold brow of youth could be). Her blue eyes were snapping with the range of her thoughts among her projects for this day. The odd little fold in the flesh at the corners was so characteristic, so significant of her fine good humor. Her whole face was so animated and . . . he didn't know what to call it but . . . Rosemaryish. And that low bubbly chuckle of hers was constantly in her throat.

His breast swelled. *Why, she is well!* he thought.

Mr. Gibson hid this for a secret temporarily while he smiled and patted all her plans on the back encouragingly . . . and said goodbye.

But he rode the bus with a joyful booming in his heart. *She is well again! Rosemary is alive and well!* He had as good as raised her from the dead.

All day long, the miracle rang in his heart. He would come back to it, back to it, and, every time, it boomed and rang like bells.

When he came home, to admire the lamb and watch her dainty hunger, and hear how the day had gone and was already only a foundation for tomorrow, he said firmly, "Tomorrow night, Rosemary, we are going to celebrate."

"Are we? Why?"

"Can you drive ten miles? Can the Ark go ten miles?"

"Why, sure it can," she said gaily. "I don't see why not."

"Then we are going out for dinner—to a restaurant I know. Out on the highway. Oh, you'll like it."

"But *why?*"

"To celebrate." He was mysterious.

"Celebrate *what,* Kenneth?"

"It's a secret," he said. "I may tell you tomorrow."

"What on earth are you talking about?"

"Never mind," he said shyly. He almost hated to share his very miracle—even with her.

In the evening of the next day (which was a Friday), the ancient car proceeded noisily out upon the highway, west of town. It rode high and old-fashioned, in a gait that was both stately and lumbering, like a stout matron who nevertheless has her dignity. Rosemary, in a new white dress with a splash of red roses on the bodice, with a big soft red wool scarf tied around the top of her, drove them without seeming to try too hard. *She is equal to this,* thought Mr. Gibson with pride, *because she is well. And there is no doubt about it.*

Mr. Gibson had gone so far as to reserve a table, for this little restaurant was very popular, both on account of its fine French cooking and its atmosphere, which was dim and smoky and smelled deliciously of sauces. It wasn't cheap either. But this was a celebration.

They drank a little wine. They ate hugely of one delectable dish after another, and Mr. Gibson teased by refusing to explain the reason for the reckless expense of this expedition. It was delightful to be together in the midst of the smoke and the savory smells and the soft buzz of other people's conversations. Mr. Gibson knew he was preening himself. He knew that Rosemary was, too. As if they were actors or masqueraders, and out of themselves and yet being themselves in a freer truer way. He couldn't help feeling on the suave side, and a bit of a gay dog. He enjoyed it. Rosemary looked as if she felt that she was rather lovely. And so she was, he decided.

At dessert time, they had a drop of brandy with their coffee. Then without warning these two people-of-the-world fell into a fit of childlike hilarity.

Just something he said, a turn of a phrase.

And Rosemary capped it.

And he extended it.

And they were off. The whole thing spiraled up. It got funnier and funnier. They were behaving like a pair of maniacs. Mr. Gibson laughed so hard he had to retreat behind his napkin. He felt himself aching. Rosemary had her hands to the red roses printed on her bodice as if she were aching too. They rocked together. Their heads bumped. *This* was an absolute riot. They shushed each other, faces red, eyes wet, and beaming, and daring each other.

People turned mildly worried faces to look at them, and *this* was the funniest thing they'd ever *seen*. And sent them off again. Nothing on earth had ever been so funny. But never could they explain *why* to anyone else. Which was extremely funny in *itself*.

Now people were smiling by contagion and staring with real curiosity. So they controlled themselves and made their mouths stiff and sipped brandy. Rosemary thought of one more word and *said* it and off they went, careening on laughter right off the earth to some other place.

It took quite a while to simmer down. But at last, just as suddenly, the little sadness fell. It was over. They mustn't try to start it up again. No. Force nothing. Sit, with the sweet contentment in their throats, the after-taste of laughter that lies so kindly on the very membranes like a salve.

"When will you tell me what we are celebrating?" asked Rosemary gravely.

"I'll tell you now." He lifted the last drop of his brandy. "We are celebrating you. Because you are well again."

Her eyes filled with tears. She didn't answer.

He said quietly, "Well, it's late. I suppose we should go."

"Yes." She fished the red wool thing from behind her. She seemed to be trembling. The waiter pulled the table away and they rose, moving slowly, as if still entranced, still sweetly remembering the food and the fun. He took the soft wide stole and held it, and she turned her back, and he folded it around her. He wanted to tuck it close around her throat, wanted her safe and warm. He couldn't help it that his hands were tender. Rosemary bent her head, and for one quick wonderful stunning moment she pressed the warm skin of her cheek caressingly upon the bare skin of his hand.

It was only a moment. It changed the whole world.

Mr. Gibson followed her to the little lobby and opened the door which the proprietor was helping to open (saying good night, saying that a bit of a fog had come up, suggesting caution). Mr. Gibson may have replied mechanically. He was absolutely stunned.

He had just discovered that he was in love with his wife Rosemary, twenty-three years his junior—but that didn't matter. Why, he was crazy about her! Now he understood what they meant by "in love." In love . . . in love . . . in love!

They stepped out into a place of strangest beauty— not like the world at all. A heavy fog but oh, how beautiful!

Rosemary stepped back to rest a moment against him. Their two bodies were all that was left of the old world and all that mattered. Everywhere, veils fell. Across the road, the fields drowsed and drowned.

"Would you rather I drove?" he asked her.

"No, no," she said. "I understand the poor old Ark. Oh, Kenneth, *isn't* it beautiful!"

There was a vibration between them and he cherished it. It was too dear and too new and much too beautiful to mention.

They got into the car. Rosemary started the noisy old engine, and backed it out of the parking slot. Mr. Gibson strained to see, and to guide her. But he hardly knew what he was seeing. She drove slowly with full caution. The big old car went steadily. The world was invisible ahead of them and vanished behind them. They were nowhere, and yet here. Together and only ten miles from home.

Mr. Gibson didn't think behind nor too far, nor too clearly, ahead, either. He only knew he was in love, and everything—everything was piercingly different and beautiful.

The sudden headlights simply *became,* as if they'd just been created. A car raced toward them, head on. He knew that Rosemary took a sudden great pull on the steering wheel. That was all he knew but a brutal noise, one flash of pain, and then from his senses the world was gone, altogether.

Chapter VI

HE WAS trussed up, he was chained, like a dog in a kennel. He could not, even if he had had the ambition to try, get out of this bed and away from the contraptions that imprisoned him.

"Then, she *is* all right?" he said. "You've actually seen her?" He tried to bend his gaze and search *this* face, but the girl with the clip-board had seated herself and was too low. He could see the top of her head, but not the eyes.

"Well, no," he heard her voice saying, "I didn't actually see her. But I was up on her floor—trying to . . . you know . . . get information? And she's all right, Mr. Gibson. Honest. Everybody's told you."

"What do you mean by 'all right'?" he queried irritably. His leg up in this undignified shocking fashion, his torso constricted somehow, his senses obstructed, the whole shock and indignity of injury upon him . . . yet he himself was "all right" in hospital parlance. What did they mean, except that he wasn't in mortal danger? (Oh, was she?)

"Told me she was out for a while and shaken up quite a bit," said the uncultivated voice, "but that's all. Now please, Mr. Gibson . . ."

He rolled his head. It seemed to be all the freedom he had. But who, he thought with a flooding woe, is going to make Rosemary smile . . . ?

"Are you in pain?" the girl said not unsympathetically. "Maybe I could come back."

"I sure am in pain," he said. "Exactly. Right inside of it. I'm in some kind of cocoon made out of fuzz and fog . . ." (Fog? His heart winced.) He must have been given drugs. His tongue felt thickened but loosened, too. "I don't feel the pain, you see, but I know it is there, all around me. And it knows I know. What day is it? What time is it? Where am I?" he jested with his frightened lips.

"It's Saturday, the twentieth of May," she told him slowly and patiently. "It's nine twenty A.M. and you are in Andrews Memorial. You were brought in last night, and honest, Mr. Gibson, *I'm* sorry but I *have* to get this information for the office . . ."

"I know," he said soberly.

He was afraid, sweating afraid, that they were all lying to him. It wasn't inconceivable. Battered and broken as he was, they might, in their wisdom, have decided to conspire and keep from him a sorrow. He opened his eyes as wide as he could and strained to lift his head and peer at this girl through the fuzz and the mist. "Sit a little higher. I can't see you," he demanded.

The girl elevated herself. She thought, Gee, he's got nice eyes. On a girl, they'd be gorgeous! Wouldn't it be, though? It's like me and my sisters all got the straight hair and the boys got the natural waves. . . . She lowered her gaze so as not to be caught with such thoughts.

"What are they *doing* to her?" Mr. Gibson said wildly.

"Why, they got her under sedation, I guess. Least I couldn't talk to her. Probably they want to watch her a few days . . ."

"That's right," he said excitedly. "Yes, that's what they must do. Keep her and watch her. You see, she hasn't been strong. She's had quite a time and this could set her back . . ."

The girl sighed and poised her pen. "I got your name and address. Now, lessee . . . When were you born, Mr. Gibson? Please, if you'll just let me get this blank filled out . . ."

"Sorry," he said. "January fifth, nineteen hundred. Which makes it entirely too easy to figure out how old I am. You don't even have to subtract, do you?"

The girl wrote "Yes" after "Married?" . . . "How long have you been married, Mr. Gibson?" she asked aloud.

"Five weeks."

"Oh, *really?*" Her voice became bright and interested. The next question on her blank was "Children?" She started to write a "No" and caught herself. "Is this your *first* wife?"

"My first . . . my only . . . Will you tell me one thing?" He fought to see her plain. "Is *she* in pain?"

"Look," the girl said, determined this time. "What can I *do,* Mr. Gibson? Honest to gosh, nobody's trying to kid you. They don't think she's even got a concussion. I'd know if there was anything bad. Believe me, I'd tell you."

He could see her face now, and it was kind and shiny and in earnest. "I believe you would," he said weakly. "Yes, thank you."

He was in a ward. There was no telephone. He was divided from Rosemary. He was farther from her than if he'd been a thousand miles. He said, whimsical in helplessness, "Could I send her a postcard?"

The girl said, "Now. Probably *she'll* be able to come down here and see you . . . at least by tomorrow."

"They might let her leave before me?" said Mr. Gibson at once, in alarm.

"Well, I should think *so*. After all, *you* got to wait a while . . ."

"They mustn't let her." He couldn't bear to think of Rosemary alone. Mrs. Violette might be hired to stay, but Mrs. Violette was so remote and cool. . . . Paul Townsend would be kind, but he couldn't be with her. There was nobody, he thought in panic— Yes. Yes there *was!* Rosemary had no people, but he had a person. *He had a sister.*

"Could you send a telegram?" he asked abruptly.

"I guess I could see to it for you, or the nurse . . ."

"*You* do it. To Miss Ethel Gibson." He gave her the address. "Are you writing it down? Send this. 'Don't worry but car accident puts me in hospital. Rosemary O.K. but we need you. Can you possibly come.' "

"Love?" the girl asked, scribbling busily.

"Love, Ken."

"Twenty words."

"Never mind. Please send it. Will you do that for me? I don't know where there is any money . . ."

"I'll see about it," she soothed. "They can charge it on your bill. Now, do you feel better? Now will you tell me the answers to all this stuff?"

So he told her the answers.

"O.K.," she said at last. "I guess I got the whole story of your life. Now, don't worry, Mr. Gibson, I'll surely send the telegram."

"You're very good . . ."

"So long." She smiled. She liked him. He was kinda cute. Didn't look to be fifty-five, either. With the kind of skin he had—fair, and stuck to his cheekbones. A woman would have had to have her face lifted already. And him married only five weeks to his first wife. She thought it was cute, and a little bit amusing. "Don't worry so much about your bride," she said affectionately.

"I'll try not," he promised. But he had received the news of her amusement and thought he would not open himself for the amusement of strangers again.

When she had gone, he thought drunkenly: Story of my life. She hadn't got *any* of it. . . . Then his whole life's story went by him in a rush, and his heart throbbed hard for the disappointment and the postponement.

But he took hold of himself and called up patience. He would heal, painfully, in time. The pain was nothing. It could be endured. He was not reconciled to the time it would take, but he would endeavor to be.

If only Rosemary had not been set back too much! If only Ethel—good reliable sister Ethel—if she could come and keep . . . keep his house! He felt sure she would respond as he himself would have responded, of course, to such a telegram. Ethel might even fly. His sister, Ethel, was not as far away from him in time as was Rosemary, upstairs. Ethel would come and take care and, in time, all would be well again.

Meanwhile, Mr. Gibson saw that the man on his right lay stupidly inert with a tube running in a disgusting way through one nostril. The man on his right had his ear upon the pillow, under which was a magic disk that poured out a soap opera. The ward was full of men all waiting as best they could . . . and most in pain. Some of them might be in love, for all he knew.

Mr. Gibson lay remembering words, for words were good to help keep off the pain—that brute and wordless thing —and to pass the time.

. . . an ever-fixèd mark
That looks on tempests and is never shaken;
It is the star to every wandering bark
Whose worth's
Unknown . . .
Unknown . . .
Unknown . . .

He seemed to sleep.

Later in that shapeless day they brought him a wire: FLYING SOONEST. ETHEL.

Mr. Gibson sighed so deeply that it made his chest ache.

"And I almost forgot. Your wife sends love," the nurse said brightly.

"Does she?"

"She was pretty anxious to know how *you* were. Let me squinch this pillow over. Is that more comfortable?"

"I am comforted," he said quaintly. "Can you send her my love?"

"We sure can," the nurse said merrily. "I'll put it on the grapevine, right away."

People are good, thought Mr. Gibson, weak with satisfaction. People are really awfully good. Good nurse. Good sister Ethel. This misery would pass.

Chapter VII

"GOOD TO COME," he said to her, the next morning. "So *very good* to come. So *glad* to see you."

"Think nothing of it, old dear," said Ethel, standing in her old familiar way, with the effect of being on both feet instead of settling her weight on one and using the other for balance, as most do. Ethel was a woman of some bulk. Although she wasn't fat, her waist was solid, her legs sturdy, her shoulders wide. She was wearing a tweedy suit of severe cut and a tailored blouse, but her short gray-threaded hair was uncovered and her square ringless hands were ungloved.

"Pretty state of affairs this is," she said in her hearty voice. She had bright brown eyes in a face that would launch no ships. (Ethel looked a good deal like their father had, he realized suddenly. Now that she was forty-seven.) "How do you feel?" she inquired.

"Don't ask me. You wouldn't want to hear about it. I want you to go to Rosemary . . ."

"I've been to Rosemary."

"You have?" He felt stunned.

"It's ten A.M. my lad," said Ethel. "And I got off that plane in the middle of the night and the milk-train or whatever I took landed me here at five A.M. I've met your landlord. I've seen your house. I've had a bath in it. And I got in to see Rosemary because *she* is in a semiprivate room, whereas all kinds of indecent things were going on in this ward, or so they implied." Ethel glanced at the man with the tube in his nostril and did not flinch.

Mr. Gibson gave out a weak "Oh," feeling somewhat flattened by her energy.

"Woke up your Mr. Townsend, I guess. Must say he was very amiable about it. When I identified myself, he let me in. Nothing to it."

"Paul's a good fellow . . ."

"Very charming," said Ethel dryly, "one of those dream-boats, eh? And a rich widower, too? My! Quite a little house you live in, Ken."

"Isn't it?"

"I put my things in what I judged to be Rosemary's room." Her wise glance understood everything.

"Yes," he said feebly. All at once, he could not imagine brisk, sensible, energetic Ethel in the little house, at all. He said impatiently—because she gave the effect of a gale blowing a sudden gust that disrupted a certain neatness and order of his thoughts— "Tell me, Ethel. How *is* Rosemary?"

"Not a scratch on her," said Ethel promptly. "She's a little unhappy. So sorry it happened. Worried about you. And so forth. I understand she was doing the driving."

"Yes, it's her car . . ." he began.

"Which car is pretty much of a mess, so Mr. Townsend tells me. I can't quite visualize . . ." Ethel frowned. "Usually it is the driver who gets the worst of it. Seems the other car hit yours right smack on the side where *you* were sitting."

"Other car . . ." Mr. Gibson winced.

"Two men in it. Neither one hurt, except superficially. *You* seem to have got the worst of it. Only a few bones broken, Ken? Sounds to me you are lucky to be alive to tell the tale."

"*I* can't tell the tale," he said testily. "*I* can't remember a thing about it."

"Just as well," said Ethel. "Spares you some interviews. It's going to be a kind of impasse, I'm afraid. Nobody will dare sue anybody."

"Sue?" He felt bewildered.

"You see, they were on the left in the fog, where they shouldn't have been. But Rosemary turned left, which was wrong of her. And the police smelled alcohol on both your breaths."

"A drop of brandy . . ." murmured Mr. Gibson sadly.

"The cops have literal minds."

"Rosemary." Mr. Gibson did not go on, discovering that all he wanted was to be saying her name.

"She's a nice girl, Ken," said his sister.

"Yes," he said relaxing.

Ethel grinned at him. Her eyes had such a wise look,

kind and indulgent. "I gather that you have been up to some good deeds."

"Well . . ."

"She couldn't say enough, Rosemary couldn't. According to her she was broke and ill and down and out. I suppose this appealed to you."

Ethel was teasing but Mr. Gibson felt dead serious. "She was badly run-down. That's exactly why I wanted you . . ."

"Drastic, wasn't it?" Ethel cocked one brow.

"What was?"

"To *marry* her."

"It may seem so . . ." he said stiffly, on the defensive.

"She's on the young side, isn't she?" his sister said. "Let's see. You are fifty-five. Well, *she* thinks you are a saint on earth—and perhaps you are." She grinned affectionately.

"I haven't," said Mr. Gibson indignantly, "the slightest intention of being a saint on earth or anywhere else—"

Ethel laughed at him. "Soft-hearted old Ken. I needn't have worried. *You'd* never take up with a blonde, now, would you? It would be a poor thing, a waif or a stray . . ."

"I'd hardly say . . ." he began.

"She's obsessed with gratitude," said Ethel, wearing now a faint frown. "Devoted to you. Of course . . ." she resettled her weight, "as I gather, she took care of her father for some years?"

"Yes, some years. She certainly did."

"Deeply attached, then," said Ethel. "And you come along. I suppose she's transferred . . ."

Mr. Gibson moved his head inquiringly.

"Father-image," said Ethel.

He lowered his eyelids.

"She claims you saved her life and reason," Ethel went on. "I wouldn't be surprised, either. It would be just like you."

"In loco parentis?" said Mr. Gibson lightly.

"That's obvious enough," said Ethel carelessly, "to anyone who knows even the rudiments of psychology. Well, good luck to you both."

"She is a dear girl," said Mr. Gibson quietly.

"I'm sure she is," said Ethel in her indulgent way. "And you are rather a dear, yourself. Well, here I am.

Got a month's leave of absence and all set to take over."

"So good," he murmured, feeling very tired.

"Your house is cute as a button, Ken, but it sure is a long haul on that bus. Give me three thousand miles on a nice safe airplane. Bus drivers are such a ruthless breed. The insensitive way they slam two tons of juggernaut through the innocent streets. Terrifies me."

"Terrifies *you!*" He rallied to tease and praise her. "Come now, not Ethel the intrepid! How are you, my dear?"

"A little fed up," she said frankly. "A little tired of the subway. In fact, Ken, I'm thinking I rather like your climate." She lifted her strong chin.

"Good," he said. "We'll make a native of you in six weeks."

"Well, we'll see. Now, what do you want? What can I bring you? What shall I do for you?"

His heart, which had shriveled a little, let go and expanded. "Be here," he begged. "Live in my house. Take care of Rosemary for me."

"Can do," said Ethel, and he relaxed against his sense of her strength. "Poor old boy," she said lovingly. "We are not—are we?—getting any younger. . . . Although you are the smart one."

"I?"

"To live as you do. Right out of the rat race. Letting the world go by. I think I'll resign from the fray myself. And acquire innocence."

"Innocence?"

"Dear old Ken," she said. "You and your poetry."

Late that very afternoon the hospital discharged Rosemary.

"After all," said Ethel cheerily, "there are so few beds and so many people so much worse off. And I am here to take care of Rosemary. If I had realized, I could have brought her clothing . . . but no matter. We'll take a taxi."

To Mr. Gibson her voice was patter . . . patter he scarcely heard. His attention was bent upon his wife Rosemary, upon the state of her body and her soul.

There she was, standing at the foot of his bed, wearing the white dress with the red flowers on it, and dirty and crumpled the dress was. She hugged around her the red stole. Her face was too pale for the strong red that wrapped her.

"Are you *sure* . . .?" said he. *He* didn't think she looked well enough to go out of the hospital.

"I'm so sorry," burst Rosemary. "So sorry! Oh, Kenneth, I wish it had been me. I'd have done anything in the world rather than hurt you . . ." She was quivering with the need to say this.

"Oh, come now," said Mr. Gibson in some alarm. "We had an accident. Now, mouse . . . it's nothing to worry about." He thought, It's set her back, alas. "Here's Ethel come all this way," he soothed . . . *"Your* sister, Rosemary." (He had to give her something. He gave her Ethel.) "The two of you are going to have a fine time." He looked as bright and easy as he could. "I just have to lie here with my leg hung up like the Monday wash—until the bones take a notion to mend. But it *will* mend—"

He had coaxed no smile. Rosemary said, "I turned to the left, you see. I thought . . ."

"You are not to blame," said Ethel a little loudly and very firmly. "There *is* no blame."

"Of course not," cried Mr. Gibson, appalled at *this*. "Of course you are not to blame! What an idea! Now, Rosemary, don't think about it. Please. Just wipe it out of your mind. Be like me. *I* don't remember a thing about it, you know. Just whammo . . . and here I am." He smiled at her.

"Don't you?" she said a little pathetically. She moistened her lips. "How do you feel?"

"I feel ridiculous," he said crisply, "and pretty undignified, believe me." But he was powerless to reach behind that white-faced stare. He feared she was still shocked, still fighting against the fact of the accident, still trying to wish it away. "Take her home, Ethel," he begged. "Now Rosemary, I want you to do as Ethel says. I want you to rest."

"Yes. I will, Kenneth. I wasn't hurt at all."

"Good night, then," he said gently. "And Ethel, you take care of her." (He thought, Oh yes, she has been hurt. She has been set back. Oh, too bad!) He said aloud, "I want you to be well, Rosemary?"

"Yes," she said. "I will be well." Just as if it was something she'd do to please him.

Then she was gone.

Ethel shepherded her charge into the taxi and then made conversation. She was sorry for this stranger, her sister-in-law. (And *in-law*, she presumed, was exactly all.) However had this poor thing got herself into such a false and ridiculous position? Her brother, Ken, was such a dreamer, such an unrealistic soul. The whole affair was pitiful. Ethel set out to comfort Rosemary.

"You really shouldn't entertain this feeling of guilt," said Ethel kindly. "There *is* no such thing as guilt, you know."

"I don't feel that exactly . . ." said the sad mouth, the low voice of Rosemary. "I feel so *sorry*. I hate so to to see him . . ."

"Of course you do," soothed Ethel. "He has done a great deal for you. I know. Just like him."

"Kenneth—" began his wife in a voice more resolute and shrill.

But Ethel cut in. "He's an old dear. But so vulnerable. Some people, of course, are like that. Charity does something for them. Expresses some need. Fills some deficiency."

Rosemary said, faintly breathless, "I love your brother very much. I think he's wonderful. I *hate*—"

Ethel looked at her and pitied her. "Naturally," she said. "We can only hate the ones we love, you know."

"But I don't hate *him*," said Rosemary. "I *couldn't. Possibly.*"

"Of course not," said Ethel. "That is the trouble. Of course, you 'couldn't possibly.' But you are still a young woman, Rosemary. That is just a fact and none of your fault. You really needn't feel guilty about it."

"But . . ."

"We understand," intoned Ethel. "We understand these things. Now. My dear, just try to relax. Just don't brood about the accident. Tell me, what are those incredible masses of flowers? Geraniums! I never saw such a sight. Now, I'm here to see that you rest and recover. Frankly, I am delighted. It makes a break for me that I have wanted for a long time. You see, I'm quite selfish, Rosemary. We all are."

"I suppose so," said Rosemary dispiritedly.

"You will soon feel strong and well . . ."

"Yes."

Ethel herself felt strong and well and pleased with the feel of the helm in her hand.

Mr. Gibson lay thinking about Rosemary. It had been a flat and almost stupid exchange between them. Lugubrious. Also conventional. Nothing like what he had wanted. But what else could it have been, here in the crowded ward, with the slack eyes of the man with the tube, the curious eyes of the man on the other side, both fixed on the spectacle of Rosemary. And Ethel, also there.

Mr. Gibson braced himself. Wait then. In no such public spot as this would he declare his love. Nor would he declare at all until he felt less unsure of himself than he felt today. What did he know about love, anyhow? He *could* have mistaken a fatherly joy for the other thing. Little enough he knew about that, either. Bachelor that he had been. (Innocent.) And of course another mistake was *quite* probable. Whatever *he* felt, Ethel could be right about Rosemary. Ethel was a shrewd and worldly woman, and her judgment deserved attention. He may have taken a gesture of loving gratitude in the wrong way entirely. *Of course* Rosemary was grateful to him. He squirmed at the thought of it. He had made her stop saying so. But that might have contributed to her—obsession, as Ethel called it. Well, he would have to be rid of *that*—be sure *that* wasn't warping and interfering. . . .

His heart was beating in slow rhythm, a kind of dirge-time.

> For should I but see thee a little moment,
> Straight is my voice hushed . . .

He felt very much aware of his broken self and the harsh truths of the hospital, the burn of the taut sheet upon his skin, the uncozy light. The scene in the restaurant was long long ago . . . the other side of the mist . . . far—and receding like a dream.

Certainly, *certainly,* the last thing he would do was upset Rosemary any more than she was upset, right now. He didn't want to upset her ever. To have one's adopted father . . . (Mr. Gibson's mind fled from finishing this thought. It was too abhorrent!) He had better swallow down what might be only some foolishness of his . . . at least for the time being. Ah, poor girl—to blame herself because she happened to be driving. But Ethel was sensible. Ethel's sound common sense would pull her out of *that. He* could not. He couldn't be there.

Mr. Gibson sighed and his ribs ached. Sometimes he felt pitiable, rather than ridiculous, to be so strapped and tied together as he was. So stopped . . . right in the midst of all he had been accomplishing. But he must endure. At least his sister Ethel had come. . . . God bless her!

Chapter VIII

DAYS BEGAN to take on shape and they went by. At first Ethel and Rosemary came together to see him every afternoon. It was not long before he ceased to look forward to this visiting hour. They spoke with such common-place cheer. They stood beside his bed and, all down the ward, others stood and spoke in the same way. Mr. Gibson felt as if he were in the zoo and human beings came here to make noises at the animals that communicated good will but little else. As if men in a hospital ward had lost their reason, their ideas, their imaginations. They were bodies healing, and nothing more.

During the second and third weeks, Ethel often came alone, saying that Rosemary was resting. And Ethel gave the cheerful trivial news. Mrs. Violette was a great expense, but they would keep her if Ken insisted. The weather was charming. Rosemary? Oh, Rosemary was being sensible, eating well, getting along fine. Mr. Gibson beat down a jealous sense that the two of them got on and the house ran too well without him. He wished he could get out of here. He didn't say so. He said he was getting along fine, too.

Paul Townsend dropped in once or twice, and spoke cheerful commonplaces. Shame this had to happen. Everyone well at home. Getting along fine.

Only when one or another of his fellow teachers came and the talk went—as it had gone so many years of his life—flitting through remembered books, did Mr. Gibson receive a sense of nourishment from the visitation.

One day, Rosemary came alone. Ethel had been speaking more and more seriously of staying on permanently. Today she had gone looking around for jobs. To Mr.

Gibson's shock, Rosemary proposed to go job-hunting herself.

"After all," she said, and she was standing on both feet, much as Ethel did, "a substitute is going to finish off your year, Kenneth, and then it is summer. You are not the richest man in the world. . . . You *shouldn't* work at anything *this* summer, after these injuries. . . . And in spite of the insurance, you know we can't recover all the cost of all of this." She looked very bleak for a moment. "But there is no reason why I can't help. I'm well now . . . "

She was *well* enough. She looked physically quite sound. He didn't know what made him fidget. He seemed to catch overtones of Ethel's briskness and practicality in Rosemary's voice . . . The new man in the right-hand bed was frankly listening to every word being said, and Mr. Gibson couldn't quite black out his own consciousness of this fact, either.

"A woman needn't be a parasite," said Rosemary, "unless, I suppose, she's married to some fabulous captain of industry who can afford a parasite . . ."

"Or *likes* them," he murmured. "Some men are old-fashioned." He revised his thought, sternly. "If you would enjoy a job," he told her, "*of course,* Rosemary. How . . . how is the garden?"

"All right, I guess."

"Have you tried to paint the little wall?" He was groping back after something far away, the other side of the fog.

"No," she said. "I haven't. I could never be a painter, Kenneth. Just a dabbler. Ethel says, you know, people go in for things like that in retreat from reality, and I'm afraid I haven't been aware enough of the . . . well, the economic world . . . the commercial world . . . the real world."

(Mr. Gibson thought to himself, Yes, this is Ethel. But it is good for her.)

"I guess I was more or less sheltered for too long," said Rosemary.

"We-ell . . ." he considered. "I dunno as I would call it *that.*" A prison is a shelter, he was thinking, in a way. But . . .

"I see now," she said vigorously. "There was something too dreamy and not quite tough enough about the

way I let things go on. If I'd had more sense . . . if I
had faced up to facts . . . I needn't have ever gotten into
such a state as I was in . . ."

"As you *were*," he said admiringly. "You sound like a
very determined young woman now."

"I am." She smiled. The praise had pleased her. "There
are jobs I could do, now."

"Yes." He knew. Jobs for rude health. First stepping-
stones toward working experience. "Well," he sighed, "I
never proposed to keep you wrapped in what the British
call cotton wool . . . forever." He looked at the detestable
ceiling.

> Curly-locks, curly-locks, wilt thou be mine?

he intoned . . .

> Thou shalt not wash dishes nor yet feed the swine,
> But sit on a cushion and sew a fine seam,
> And feed upon strawberries, sugar and cream.

He'd made her laugh. (If the laugh was a bit artificial, a bit strained, perhaps this was because the man in
the next bed was wearing such a look of shocked con-
tempt on his whiskery face.)

"What an unbalanced diet!" cried Rosemary, attempt-
ing to be gay.

"Much too rich and probably fattening," Mr. Gibson
agreed, looking drowsy. Covertly he inspected her new
briskness. Was it real? Was it Rosemary? Was he *wrong*
to so dislike it?

"Do you need more books?" she said suddenly. "I wasn't
sure . . ."

He squirmed his head. "It's an effort to hold a book, I
find," he said miserably. "Maybe I have had too steady a
diet of poetry. When 'life is real, life is earnest'—and
there I go." His own smile felt somewhat artificial.

"Ethel has told me so much about you," said his wife.
"How you always have helped people—"

"Oh, now . . ." he sputtered. He disliked this kind of
pious judgment. Like everybody, he had only and ever
tried to be comfortable.

"Just the same," said Rosemary resolutely, "Ethel and
I are going to take care of *you*, for a change."

(Mr. Gibson didn't like the sound of this, one bit. But, he thought, perhaps she needed to get rid of the burden of gratitude and if this was her way, he would have to bear it.) So he told her, *willing* his eyes to twinkle, that he fancied this would be delightful.

After she had gone, he gave the back of his head to his curious neighbor, and mused on this meeting. Rosemary's vigor and resolution, he perceived, was a strain upon her. She was pressing herself to be something she had never been. But perhaps now needed to be? Well, if she needed to feel useful to him and this was her way, why, *he* must acquire the grace to receive.

He would just have to shuck off his sense of dismay, the illogical notion that he had *been* receiving, formerly, and now lost something precious. If Rosemary saw duty, why, *he* should understand this. *He* had seen duty and enjoyed the doing of it, often enough. He must obliterate this baseless feeling that something . . . some hidden thing . . . was very wrong within Rosemary. After all, he mused in sad whimsicality, if man cannot live by bread alone, neither can woman be satisfied by cream and strawberries.

He tried to keep from his old habit of quoting in his mind. Too many poems were about love. Maybe *all* of them. . . .

Mr. Gibson had a bit of a shock one day, when he discovered that some badly smashed bones in his thigh had grown back together somewhat awkwardly. Unless he wished to go through a series of attempts at bonebreaking and repairing that would be expensive (and no results guaranteed) he would be lame.

He said, to Ethel, to Rosemary, this was not important. It did not really matter if he limped a little.

But when he tried to walk, when he realized how he *must* limp, henceforth . . . it mattered some.

At last he went home. Ethel came to fetch him in a taxi. Rosemary kept the hearth: she met him at the cottage door. Still on crutches, Mr. Gibson swung himself into the living room, eager for the sense of home upon his heart.

It did not come. The colors looked a bit on the cute side. The furniture was obviously "furnished" furniture. What he remembered so fondly must have been totally subjective. Surely there were also subtle displacements. Chairs stood at other angles. He sat down, feeling pain.

Jeanie Townsend came to the door bearing flowers and greetings, and everyone had to pretend that the little house was not already bestrewn to capacity with flowers. But the child was welcome. She helped, with her presence and her good manners, this moment to go over all their heads and pass.

Then, her father ambled in after her, wearing his leisure clothes. The white T-shirt tight to his fine muscular torso set off the deep tan of his arms and neck. After the hospital ward, he was almost offensively healthy and powerful.

"Darn shame," said he, as he had already said twice before in the hospital, "a thing like this has to happen. Guess we never know, do we? Oh thanks, Rosie."

Rosemary was serving tea with trembling hands.

"I guess you'll be well taken care of, like me," grinned Paul, "by a regular flock of females." His big brown hands were startling upon a frail cup and saucer.

"Waited on hand and foot," said Mr. Gibson, accepting with his pale claw a slab of pound cake from Ethel. (She had always considered this a great delicacy, but Mr. Gibson rather enjoyed, although of course it wasn't *wise*, some frosting on a cake.)

"That reminds me," said Ethel, "speaking of waiting on . . . About Mrs. Violette, Ken. She *isn't* worth what she is costing."

"If both of you are going into trade," said Mr. Gibson mildly, "who is going to wait on me, hand-and-foot, then, pray tell?"

"But we aren't going yet," said Rosemary quickly. "Not until you are perfectly well again." She was sitting on the edge of a chair and her attitude was like that of a new servant in a new situation, too anxious to find her place, and to please. He longed to say to her, "Sit back, Rosemary. This is your house."

Ethel was speaking. "Even so, when we do go off to work, Ken . . . I *don't* like the idea of a foreigner left to her own devices. They all need supervision. They have little extravagances, you know. Things disappear from the icebox." Her somewhat craggy face was rather amused by human frailty.

Jeanie said, "We've had Mrs. Violette for more than a year. She keeps everything so clean . . ."

"Ah," said Ethel, "but there's only you, dear. Your poor grandmother—whereas, here . . . why, there is nothing to keeping a house like this. I've kept my apartment *and* held a job for years. And with two of us to share off . . . both grown and able-bodied. Be a cinch."

Paul said, "Rosie's fine, now."

Jeanie's eyes glistened. "I like Mrs. Violette," she said.

"A waste," said Ethel. "I *prefer* doing for myself."

Mr. Gibson, munching pound cake, knew with a pang that it would be impossible for him even to ask his sister Ethel how long she proposed to live in his house. After she had come so promptly, so generously, giving up all she had been doing for his and Rosemary's sake? He could not *ever* suggest that she had better go. Mrs. Violette would go, instead.

So the chairs would stand at angles that subtly annoyed him. The menu would include pound cake and certain other dishes. Rosemary wouldn't be mistress of her own house, not quite. Ethel would sleep in the second bed in Rosemary's room.

He was ashamed. He wrenched at his thoughts. How mean he was! How petty, selfish! (What a fool he was, too!) Thirty-two from fifty-five leaves twenty-three, and no matter how many times he tried the arithmetic, he never got a better answer.) He had his place, his own bed he had made, cozy among his books.

Ingrate! Here in this pleasant cottage, with two devoted women, both anxious to "take care" of him, why could he not count his blessings and give over, forever . . . wipe out and forget a foolish notion that he, Kenneth Gibson, was destined to love a woman and be loved, on any but the present terms? *Which were fine* . . . he shouted at himself inside his head. Admirable! His days would be sunny with kindness and good will and mutual gratitude.

Paul Townsend got up and stretched. He couldn't seem to help exuding excess health. He said he had to go, he'd left off in the middle of trimming his ivy. "And by the way, Rosie," he said with his warm smile, "if you really want some cuttings there are going to be millions of them."

Rosemary said, "Thanks so much, Paul, but I don't suppose I'll have the time . . ."

"Of course you'll have the time!" cried Mr. Gibson, shocked. "Don't let *me* be in the way . . ."

She only smiled and Paul said he'd save a few dozen in water anyhow, and Jeanie, who had been seen but not heard most of this time, as she got up to go, said sweetly, "I'm *awfully* glad you are home again, Mr. Gibson."

By the tail of his eye, Mr. Gibson perceived on Ethel's face a look he knew very well. It was the look she wore when she was *not* going to say what she was thinking. This was fleetingly disturbing. In just that moment, Mr. Gibson felt quite out of touch.

"Forgot," said Paul in the doorway. "Mama sends regards and all that. Say, why don't you hob—come on over and sit with her sometimes. Gibson? She'd love it."

"I may do so, some day," said Mr. Gibson as cordially as he could, and Rosemary let the Townsends out.

"They have been so nice," she said returning. "More tea, Kenneth?"

"No, thank you." Mr. Gibson dug about in his head for a topic to mention aloud. "Jeanie is a quiet one, isn't she? Nice child."

"I don't suppose she's especially quiet with her contemporaries," Ethel said. "Although she certainly does sit like a cat watching the mouse. . . . Deeply attached to her father. Unconsciously, of course, she's scared to death he might marry again."

"Why do you say that?" inquired Mr. Gibson.

"She's bound to be," said Ethel. "And of course, he will. That's inevitable. Man in his prime and a very attractive man to women, or so I imagine. And well off, too. I doubt if he can help himself. Some blonde will catch him." Ethel took up the last piece of pound cake. "I presume he is actually only waiting for the old lady to die. Although until he gets Jeanie launched off to school or into a romance of her own, he may sense there would be trouble from that quarter."

"Trouble?" said Rosemary politely.

"The inevitable jealousy," said Ethel. "A teenager, especially, can be so bitter against a step-parent."

"I don't know Jeanie very well," murmured Rosemary rather unhappily.

"They don't intend to be known, these teen-agers," Ethel said. "They like to think they are pretty deep." She hooted.

They weren't too deep for her, the quality of its tone implied.

Mr. Gibson had known quantities of young people as they filtered through his classrooms. But the relationship, there, he reminded himself, was an arbitrary thing. They were supposed to respect him, on the surface at least. He had had many bright chattering sessions listening to the tumble of their inquiring thoughts. They'd show off to teacher. He would be the last to know them in a private or social capacity. He said rebelliously, nevertheless, "They *feel* deep."

"Don't we all?" said Ethel with one of her wise glances. "Shall I tell you whom I am sorry for?" she continued. "That's old Mrs. Pyne, poor soul."

"I don't feel as if I know her well enough to be sorry or otherwise," continued Mr. Gibson, for this was at least talk.

"Isn't it obvious?" said Ethel. "That to be old and ill and dependent upon, of all things, a son-in-law, is a pretty dismal fate? I see them wheel her out on that front porch of theirs every day and there she sits in the sun. Poor old thing. She must know, whether she lets herself admit it or not, that she is a nuisance. She must know it'll be a relief to all concerned when she dies. If ever I get old and helpless," said Ethel forcefully, "me for an institution. Remember that."

"I'll make a note of it," said Mr. Gibson with a touch of asperity. But he was doing anguished sums in his head. Take twenty years. Rosemary would be fifty-two, not many years older than Ethel was right now, and no one could be more the picture of strength than Ethel. But then he, Kenneth Gibson, would be seventy-five . . . ancient, decrepit, possibly ill . . . possibly—oh, Lord forbid!—another Professor James. Then would Rosemary be waiting for *him* to die?

He said wearily, "I'm afraid I had better lie down for a while. I'm sorry."

They sprang to assist him to his own place, where, on his own couch, among his books—his long beloveds—he tried to rest and remember without pain the bleak, the stricken pity on Rosemary's face.

One of his legs simply was not the same length as the other one. He could never conquer that little lurch in his body. He was lame. Old. Done for. So he was.

Chapter IX

LIFE IN THE COTTAGE fell quickly into a pattern. Some weeks later Mr. Gibson mused upon this. One should, he perceived, kick like a steer (if steers really do kick) in the first hour of any regime, because habit is so easily powerful and it is so soon too late.

Surely his sister Ethel had not meant to dominate. She was too fair and reasonable a person. But she had long been used to independence, to making decisions. He supposed he had been too physically weak (and too emotionally preoccupied) to notice what was happening. Of course Rosemary did not seem to think it her place to assert herself, for she was so abysmally grateful. Grateful to him. Grateful to Ethel.

However it had come about, the hours they kept were Ethel's hours. They ate on an early schedule, which made the mornings too short and too full of petty detail. Afternoons were consecrated to naps and too soon thereafter to the preparation of their early dinner. The menus reflected Ethel's preferences if only because she had them and both the Gibsons were too amiable and too flexible.

Evenings they spent *à trois*. These were long and dedicated to music, Ethel's choice—all severely classical, and sometimes listened to in learned solemnity. Or they conversed, about the music, Ethel leading. Ethel had many opinions and it was difficult not to listen and agree. Mr. Gibson hated arguments.

Then, Ethel liked a game of chess. Rosemary did not play. Once Mr. Gibson tried reading aloud for half an hour, but when Ethel capped the reading with a sharp and knowledgeable sketch of Mr. Browning as a Victorian lady's man, while he couldn't dispute the truth of all she said it yet made such a ridiculous picture in Mr. Gibson's mind that he put the book back upon the shelf with apologies to an old friend.

In fact he now lived with his sister Ethel.

Ethel in her long years in New York had got out of the habit of expecting social gatherings. Ethel reveled in being

one of three. For her, this was a crowd. They had few
callers. Paul Townsend, or Jeanie, dropped in once
and again. Their visits were not especially stimulating. Paul
was casual. Jeanie was all manners.

Mr. Gibson's old acquaintances did not drop in. He
seemed divorced from the college completely, so far out
in this little house, and all the work going on without him.

So he lived with Ethel, and Rosemary was there in
the same house. For instance, it was, quite properly, his
sister, Ethel, and not the comparatively new, the stranger
female, who attended to what nursing Mr. Gibson needed,
for she, of course, was better able to cope with certain
physical indecencies. . . .

Mr. Gibson had begun to feel that he was in a soft but
inescapable trap. He was unable to fight out of it. He
didn't know that he ought to try. Rosemary deferred to
Ethel in all things. Rosemary did not seem to want to be
alone with him. He sometimes wondered whether anything
was amiss with Rosemary. Oh, she was well and busy, willing and agreeable . . . but he and she seemed locked
away from communication and he, covering his seething
doubts, wore the same armor of perfect courtesy.

Mr. Gibson sat in the sunny living room one morning,
which was where he tended to sit. He did not often sit
out of doors, where Mrs. Pyne was to be seen a lonely
figure in her wheel chair on the Townsends' porch. He had
found he did not enjoy it. Perhaps the light was too cruel,
and fell too harshly from the sky. Perhaps he had become
used to a more cloistered effect and in physical weakness
preferred it. At any rate, he sat indoors and thought to
himself, this morning, that he had never met anything so
grueling, so nearly maddening, as this adult atmosphere of
mutual forebearance and perfect meaningless harmony.

While he pondered ways and means of rebellion, with
only half a heart that ached obscurely but all the time,
Mrs. Violette was dusting. (Both Ethel and Rosemary had
asked him whether he minded, and he had said of course
he did not mind.) He watched her swift coordinated
motion with a little idle pleasure. There was no air of good
will about Mrs. Violette particularly. She did her job, in
her cool silent way, not caring whether he minded. She
rather refreshed him. She was shifting the ornaments on
the mantelpiece when she suddenly seemed to become
aware of something behind her. She jerked her head around

and with that abrupt movement the cloth in her hand flicked out at a small blue vase and it fell. It smashed.

"Oh dear," said Ethel, who had come in on quiet feet, "and that belongs to Mr. Townsend."

"We can find another," said Mr. Gibson automatically.

Mrs. Violette ducked down and began to pick up the pieces. He noted the easy crouch of the knee, the slim straight back.

Ethel said, "Such a lovely blue! Didn't I speak of that only yesterday?"

"I didn't mean to do it," spat Mrs. Violette with an astonishing burst of anger.

"Of course you didn't mean to do it," said Ethel soothingly. "You couldn't help it."

Mr. Gibson watching Mrs. Violette's face found himself beginning to blink. Why was she so furious?

Rosemary came, called from her bedroom by the noise, "Oh, too bad . . . I don't suppose it costs much, do you?"

Ethel said, "No, no, I've seen them in the dime store. It's not expensive."

"Please don't worry about it, Mrs. Violette," said Rosemary at once. "I just hope you haven't cut yourself."

"No ma'am," said Mrs. Violette, rising. She looked boldly at Ethel for a moment. "I'll pay for it." she said contemptuously. She walked across the room with the bits of pottery in her hand and disappeared into the kitchen.

"We can't let her pay for it," said Mr. Gibson, "when it was just an accident."

Ethel was smiling a peculiar smile. "She seems to know it was no accident," she said musingly. "How odd!"

"What do you mean, no accident?" said Mr. Gibson in surprise.

"She did it because she dislikes me, of course."

"Ethel . . . !"

"She does, you know. And I did admire the color of that vase in her hearing only yesterday. She dislikes me because *I* check up on her, which is more than either of you seem to do."

"But . . . what need . . . ?" he said bewildered.

"What need? Oh me," sighed Ethel seating herself. "I believe a servant could steal you blind and you'd never know, either of you."

Mr. Gibson felt like a Babe-in-the-Wood. Such a thought had never occurred to him.

"I don't think she'd steal," said Rosemary in a low voice, hesitantly. "Do you, Kenneth?"

"Of course not!" he exploded.

"Of course not," mocked Ethel. "No 'of course not' about it. These foreigners don't have the same ideas of honesty as you do. *She* wouldn't call it stealing . . . but you would, and so would I."

"What has she stolen?" said Rosemary, looking a bit flushed.

"She takes food," said Ethel, looking mysterious. "All foreigners take food. They don't think of it as property."

"She eats," said Rosemary. "That is true."

They were in conflict. Mr. Gibson held his guilty delighted breath.

"Nor any small loose-lying thing," Ethel went on, drawling. "Don't you ever take precautions, you dear sheltered people? Don't you believe in the fact of theft? I hate to think what would happen to you in less bucolic places. There is wickedness in this world."

"Really," said Mr. Gibson much annoyed. "I see no more reason to believe that Mrs. Violette would steal than to believe she broke that vase on purpose. And I was right here, Ethel. I *saw* what happened."

"You think you did," said Ethel, as to a very young child.

He felt shaken.

"It's the first thing she has broken," began Rosemary. "She's been quite remarkable . . ."

"Quite so," said Ethel with satisfaction. "Of course, it is the first thing. Don't you see she resents me, and has, since the moment I came? So she breaks something *I* liked. I am not *blaming* her. I merely understand."

Mr. Gibson had a faint sense of something fading out of his peripheral vision. "For heaven's sakes, Ethel," he sputtered. "Anyone can have an accident!"

"There is no such thing as an accident," said Ethel calmly. "Honestly, Ken, you *are* ignorant in some fields. Subconsciously she wanted to spite me. She likes to be let entirely alone the way *you* let her be. But, of course, *I* am not such an easy mark."

"What on earth are you saying?" said Mr. Gibson in amazement. "Of course, there is such a thing as an accident. She turned to look because *you* startled her . . . and then her hand . . ."

"Oh no," said Ethel.

"Wait a minute." Mr. Gibson turned to see what might be on Rosemary's face but Rosemary was no longer in the room. She was gone. It was disconcerting.

Mr. Gibson turned back and said severely, "I don't agree with your suspicions, Ethel."

"Suspicions?" sighed Ethel, "or normal precautions? The fact is, old dear," she continued affectionately, "all of us can't live in a romantic, poetical and totally gentle world. Some of us have to face things as they are." Her bright eyes were direct and honest and he feared they were wise. "Face reality," she said.

"What reality?" he snapped.

"Facts," said Ethel. "Malice, resentment, self-interest— the necessities of the ego—all the real driving forces behind what people do. The conscious mind, old dear, is only the peak of the iceberg. You believe so easily in the pretty surfaces . . ."

"*I* do!"

"Yes, you," said Ethel kindly. "You don't know a tenth of what goes on, Ken. Your head's in the clouds. Always has been. Of course I love you *for* it. . . . But for every saint with his head in the clouds," sighed Ethel, "I suppose there has to be somebody to take the brunt of things as they really are."

"I see no reason," said Mr. Gibson with stubborn lips, "to mistrust Mrs. Violette."

"You wouldn't see a reason to mistrust anyone," said Ethel indulgently, "until the deed popped up and hit you in your nice fastidious nose. You have always sidestepped the nasty truths of this earth, brother dear. More power *to* you."

He stared at her.

"Oh, I'm sorry," she said, and she did look sorry, "I shouldn't say these things . . ."

"Why not?" he cried, "if you believe them."

But Ethel evaded and said, "You are a lot like Mama was, you know? I think you should have been the woman, Ken, and I should have been born the man."

"Tell me," he cried. "What are you saying?"

"You musn't pay any attention. Your world of poetry and quixotic goodness and faith and all the rest is a pretty darned nice place. . . ."

"And *your* world?" he demanded. "I imagine you call *it* the real world," he said, goaded to some anger.

Ethel responded to the anger. "Mine?" She looked him in the eye. "It happens to be full of knives-in-the-back and all kinds of human meannesses. It cannot help but be. Men *are* animals, whether *you* like it or not."

"And you say," he groped back for something solid with which to challenge her, "That Mrs. Violette broke the blue vase deliberately?"

"Of course, she didn't consciously plan it," said Ethel. "You don't understand. But she did break it to displease me, just the same."

"I don't believe it," said Mr. Gibson.

"Don't then," said Ethel. "Stay as sweet as you are . . . that's in a song, isn't it?" She grinned at him and he knew her teasing was a form of apology. "You are a lamb, Ken, and everybody loves a lamb. I cannot help it if I am no lamb, you know. Now, I haven't upset you, have I?"

He thought he felt as upset as he had ever felt in his life. He scarcely knew why, but he was afraid for Rosemary. So he struggled up, and, using his cane, he limped into the kitchen.

Mrs. Violette was briskly washing the counter. Rosemary was there too, just staring out the window. He thought she looked rather lonely.

"Now, Mrs. Violette," he said, "please understand that *I* will pay for the vase. It wasn't your fault."

Mrs. Violette shrugged and said nothing.

Rosemary said in a brisk voice, "Mrs. Violette tells me she has to leave us, Kenneth. She's going away with her husband, next week."

"Is that so?" he said unhappily.

"Yeah, we're taking off to the mountains," said Mrs. Violette. "He's going after a new job for the both of us. If we get it, we'll stay on up there."

"On a ranch," said Rosemary. "How nice that will be!" She sounded rather desperately cheerful. "But we'll miss you, Mrs. Violette."

Mrs. Violette made no response. She didn't care whether she'd be missed. She wasn't even angry at Ethel any more, for all Mr. Gibson could see.

"Ought we to try to get somebody else?" said he across to Rosemary worriedly.

"No," she said. "No. I'm able. Ethel and I can manage beautifully." He couldn't read her eyes *at all*.

"But if one day," he said, "Ethel were to go and live on her own, then . . ."

"Oh, she musn't do that!" cried Rosemary. "That would be a shame! Your only sister, Kenneth, and so good to come . . ." He saw her hands on the round wood of the kitchen chair. The knuckles were blue-white. "Such a fine person," Rosemary said. "So wise and so good."

Mr. Gibson felt alarmed. Something *was* wrong with Rosemary. She was a stranger and far away and how could he tell what was the matter when she seemed shut up against him . . . when her eyes seemed to search his so . . . could it be? . . . fearfully. Ethel was right, he conceded. There must be a good deal going on that he missed. He felt lost. What anxiety, what stress could there be, to so inhabit Rosemary's eyes? "Yes," he said absently. "Of course she is."

Meanwhile, Mrs. Violette scrubbed vigorously at the sink there in the small room. Ethel came in and said jauntily, "Lunch, dears? I'll start the vegetables."

Out in the yard, Paul Townsend was working near the low stone wall. He was on vacation. School was out; Jeanie was around and about; Mrs. Pyne sat on the porch. There was no privacy.

Chapter X

MR. GIBSON retired to the privacy of his own skull where he made plans.

This mysterious distress in Rosemary was intolerable. Therefore, first, he would find out what troubled her. Then, he would see to it that whatever it was troubled her no more. He felt much better, as soon as this course became plain and imperative.

He was determined, however, that he would not seek this information from Ethel, although, curiously, he was quite sure Ethel would know all about it, for he conceded that Ethel *was* wise and much more alert than he. But no. He would find out what bothered Rosemary in the simplest possible way. He would ask her. But he would do it in private.

Very well, then. This very evening he would struggle out of the hypnosis of routine. When Ethel announced bedtime, as she was so often the one to do (and night falling, and no company coming, the world still) he would not let her "tuck him in," which habit she retained although he no longer needed anyone's help in getting to bed. He would tell Ethel to go to bed herself, but he would ask Rosemary to stay. He would say to Ethel, "Ethel, I want to talk to Rosemary alone. Do you mind?"

She couldn't say she minded. Why should she mind? It would be so simple. Even as he told himself these things Mr. Gibson received a preview in his imagination. He saw Ethel's smile . . . the wise indulgent and rather amused expression she would wear, as she would nod, as she would say, "Of course I don't mind," and he knew he shrank from the prospect.

She would wear the same look that girl in the hospital had worn. Why was it so "cute" or even a little bit funny that he was fond of his wife? Come now, it was ridiculous to be this sensitive. Well, he would *act,* then. And when they were alone, how could he reach out to Rosemary, and reachieve her confidence?

He hobbled back into the living room after lunch, busy turning in his mind what words he could say, how gentle he would be, but how insistent This was the hour of his siesta, but today he did not go at once into his study-bedroom to close the blinds and lie quietly upon the bed for the accustomed period. Today, he stood looking out the east window, across the driveways, seeing, but not noticing, Paul Townsend's bare torso bending and moving there at the edge of his back lawn in some gardening activity—to which he passionately devoted his vacation days.

He could hear, but did not pay attention to, the women's voices in the kitchen. He knew Mrs. Violette was ironing, that Rosemary and Ethel were clearing away the dishes, all in the routine.

He stood in the midst of routine, plotting how he would break it, when he heard Rosemary's voice go suddenly high and full of passion and protest. He heard only the emotion, not the sense of what she said.

Then the kitchen door banged. He saw Paul Townsend straighten and lift his head. He saw Rosemary come stumbling, slowly and distractedly, into as much of the scene as he could see.

Saw Paul drop his long-handled weeder and go quickly toward her.

Saw his head bending solicitously.

Saw that Rosemary was violently weeping.

Saw Paul lift his arms.

Saw her sag, as if it were impossible not to do so, into their embrace.

Mr. Gibson wrenched his head and turned away. He could see nothing. The living room was dark, dark as night, to his light-struck eyes. He must have made some sound, for he heard Ethel say, "What's the matter?" He knew she was there in the room and he knew that she went to look briefly out of the window behind him before he felt her strong hand under his elbow.

She guided him into his own place . . . for he felt so stricken he needed guidance. But after a moment or two Mr. Gibson's sight cleared and he was quite calm and extraordinarily free. He sat down in his leather chair and laid his cane on the floor carefully. "What did you say to make her cry like that?" he asked quietly.

Ethel clamped her mouth tight for a moment. "Never mind, dear. Never mind," she said rather softly. "It's just that Rosemary insists upon misunderstanding some perfectly simple remark of mine. She thinks I meant to reproach her . . . as if I would. Of course she's emotional . . ." Ethel touched his knee, "just now. Ah Ken. I'm sorry we saw what we saw. I don't think it meant very much. Not yet."

"Yet?" he said shrewdly.

His sister drew a sigh from her shoesoles. "Ken, I am sorry to say so, but you were so foolish . . ."

"Was I? But what I wanted to do . . ." he organized his thought painfully (he cast out the phrase "in the first place") "was to make her well," he finished.

"So you have, I'm sure," said Ethel, with kind eyes. "But did you never look ahead to afterward? Didn't you realize that Rosemary, *well*, would not be the same girl?"

"I know."

"She is young. At least, comparatively . . ."

"I know. I knew that."

"When she was so ill," said Ethel, "she felt old. But she is not old. Nor does she feel old any more."

Mr. Gibson resented the kindergarten simplicity of this. "I *know*," he repeated.

"But the foolish thing, my poor Ken . . . was to bring her here—next door to such a man. A man who even shares a hobby with her! You have practically arranged for this to happen, you know."

Mr. Gibson couldn't assimilate his new thoughts. Thoughts like this had come nowhere near his mind before. Rosemary and Paul! He said, "Then they . . . they . . . ?"

"They've been friendly. Now, Ken, Rosemary is a good girl and devoted to you. But she is younger . . ."

(*I know*, screamed Mr. Gibson inside his head.)

"And he is just the right age for her and a most attractive man. I think I could have prophesied," Ethel said sadly.

Mr. Gibson sat still and contemplated folly. Folly to rent *this* little house? *He* could never have prophesied. Ideas like *this* had not entered his mind.

"Like all handsome men," Ethel went on, "he is a little bit spoiled, I suppose. Careless. He wouldn't have the self-discipline *not* to be charming. He can't help exuding that physical magnetism. Poor Rosemary. You mustn't blame her, either. There is no blame. She'd have no way of knowing how she would be drawn. The body dictates. These things are beyond one's control really. My dear, you ought to move away at once."

But Mr. Gibson contemplated his crime.

He had cheated her after all. He had given lip-service to his foreboding of this. (Yes, he *had* prophesied! Now he remembered . . . although too easily, selfishly, and in such foolish delight, he had forgotten all about it.) Of course, he could not blame Rosemary.

"I don't blame her," he said aloud.

"There is no such thing as blame," said Ethel gently. "Once you understand. She simply could not have helped herself."

"She must be . . ." He could imagine Rosemary's pain. "But does Paul . . ."

"Frankly," said Ethel, as if she had been being anything else, "I don't know how much he is attracted to Rosemary. She's not beautiful, of course, but very nice-looking and quite a lady. She is also so *near*. Propinquity is such a force."

Rather drearily Mr. Gibson supposed to himself that it was. *He* had no doubt that Paul was attracted to her.

"From his point of view," said Ethel looking shrewd, "there will be, as I say, the difficulty about the daughter. Oh, I've seen Jeanie watching Rosemary."

So had Mr. Gibson, now that he thought of it. Jeanie was so quiet, sat so still in a room, watching everyone.

"There's the old lady, too," Ethel went on. "Paul's in no position to dash gaily into . . . well, let's call it romance. . . . Move away, Ken. Rosemary is essentially loyal. It may not be too late."

"Yes, it is," said he. He had remembered something. He had been puzzled at the time. Rosemary, standing in the living room, saying with such brooding fervor ". . . never known it was possible to have so good a time. . . ." And the occasion—had it not been the first evening she and Paul Townsend had ever spent in each other's company? Wisps, he supposed, of attraction spinning between them, even then. Oh, how inevitable it had been! He saw himself—old—and now lame.

"If you want to keep her," Ethel said, "I know you are *very* fond of her. And Rosemary is *deeply* . . ."

"I'm fond of her," he said grimly, cutting off the detestable word "grateful" before it could offend his ears once more. "But I have no intention of . . . how shall I put it? . . . collecting for services rendered."

"You are very wise," said Ethel.

"Especially," he said rather primly, "since we discussed the possibility of divorce before the wedding."

"Ah then . . ." Ethel sighed and her face brightened. "I'm very glad. Then she knows she can be free if that seems best? Well . . . this puts a different light on the matter. You and I could make do," she added thoughtfully.

"Yes," he said.

"It's not a bad life. We'd have our work. We'd be rather cozy, out of the fray. One should plan one's old age, Ken. And neither of us with chick nor child. Perhaps we ought to stick together."

"Perhaps," he agreed.

"Not *here*, of course."

"No."

"If Rosemary and Paul Townsend were to marry . . ."

"No," he said conquering the shudder that threatened to destroy his poise completely, "certainly not here."

"I wouldn't be precipitous, however," Ethel warned. 'If Paul is not . . . That is, if the thing's one-sided. Rosemary might need us."

"She needs to be rid of her obligations," he said harshly. 'Or how can she know surely . . . ?"

"You are so right," said Ethel warmly. "And when you are generous and Rosemary is honorable, as I'm sure she is, why, there's no problem."

(He knew there was a little problem all his own. But he'd take care of that.)

"She'll come to you, one day," said Ethel, "when she finds the courage. I can't tell you how relieved I am, old dear, to know that you went into this with your eyes open. I've been a little bit afraid for you. A late-blooming romance can be so devastating to a born bachelor. Now then, can you sleep a little?"

"I think so," lied Mr. Gibson valiantly.

He lay on the top of his bed. He couldn't bear to imagine, from Rosemary's point of view, her dilemma. He tried to contemplate his old age.

But on another level, his plan beat in his mind. First find out what troubles Rosemary. Then, see to it that it troubles her no more.

What is love? he thought at last with a sick descending and a thud of certainty. What is hers for *me?* Not my physical magnetism, heaven knows. A lame old crock. A limping horror. The fact is, I *have* her love, as much as I am going to get. She's fond of me. But my love for her must set her free.

He lay there half an hour or more before he remembered, with a tiny crash of dismay in his brain, that Paul Townsend was a practicing Catholic, and Mr. Gibson was not so sure that divorce would be enough.

Chapter XI

THREE DAYS WENT BY. Rosemary did not come to him. She had recovered herself. She was just the same.

He did not press her to come, or to tell her anything. He began to be afraid that she never would.

Next door, Paul Townsend worked in his garden, care lessly healthy and happy and strong and visible. Old Mr Pyne sat on the porch. Young Jeanie flitted in and out The cottage ran on, exempt from life and change, in tha spurious harmony.

Mr. Gibson spent much time alone with a book open He contemplated his innocence.

Ethel was right. He did not know one-tenth of what went on. He was ignorant in most fields. Modern psycholo gical theories were to him just theories, to play games with He'd *believed* in the poetry. Honor. Courage. Sacrifice Old-fashioned words. Labels, for nothing? Oh, long ago, he had hidden himself in books, in words, but not the harsh words of fact. Poetry! Why? Because he was too thin-skinned and not brave enough to bear realities. He had not faced facts. He did not even know what they were. He must lean on Ethel, until he learned more.

He had been strangely innocent, now he saw. . . . Social-ly innocent. He had derived a good deal of innocent pleas-ure from the fact that students and teachers spoke to him on the campus paths, or in a corridor, or sometimes even on a street of the town. A nod, a greeting, a murmur of his name, had secured to him his identity. (I am not lost in eternity. I am Mr. Gibson of the English Department and there are those who know it.)

But he had had enough of people in the course of a day. His captive audiences, his classes, had permitted him the exercise of his voice. Then there were office hours during which he sometimes talked to students with kind-ness, with optimism for them, and only the most meager precautions against their guile and their flattery and their showing off had been enough. So he had felt a fullness in his days, and a shy trust in the near little world; and his privacy, his solitude, had seemed natural and pleasant and not limited. Actually he had lived a most narrow, a most sheltered, a most innocent life. He knew very little about "reality."

This must be how he had come to do, at the age of fifty-five, so stupid, so wicked, so foolish a thing. He had mar-ried a sick defenseless dependent trusting Rosemary. On the ridiculous premise that it would be an "arrangement." He now looked back upon the joyful early days with pity for his own blithe ignorance. The facts of flesh. The facts of propinquity. He had ignored all facts in a cloud of omantic nonsense. Yes, the romantic sentimental silly otion that he would be a healer! What ego! Then, worse, ow could he have thought, ever, for one moment, that his quixotic marriage could turn into a love match? *That* had been impossible from the beginning, and set forth in plain arithmetic. Thirty-two from fifty-five leaves twenty-three and ever would.

He was her father . . . emotionally. He was help, kindness, protection, and she loved him for all this, as he knew. What frightened him now was the possibility that Rosemary might go on with her bargain, until he was ancient, and never tell even herself how she wished that he would die. Rosemary might undertake to endure. She *had* endured eight years with the old professor.

She would not want to hurt him. Why, she had felt almost distracted with grief there in the hospital when she had blamed herself for so trivial a thing as his broken bones. She would neither hurt him nor break her obligations. She would freeze in loyalty and cheat herself. It was possible she did not know (or let herself know) why she had gone so naturally into Paul's arms.

The more he thought about Paul and his virtues, which were many, the more Mr. Gibson felt sure that Ethel was right. Rosemary had fallen, or was going to fall, in love with *him*, who could not possibly represent her father, but was of her own generation, virile, charming, good and kind. She could not help it.

He perceived that Rosemary had better never know a thing about *his* foolishness, for what would be the good if she knew? Pity did not interest Mr. Gibson in the least. He wanted none of it. So he banished his love, exiled it forever from his heart. He would think no more about *that.*

He retreated deliberately. He seemed to absorb himself in reading and writing. He tried not to notice . . . which might help him not to care . . . where Rosemary was or what she was doing. If he felt depressed, he told himself this was nobody's fault but his own and it would pass.

One day he found a stanza:

The gentle word, the generous intent
The decent things that men can do or say
All these to gladden her I freely spent
But could not touch her when she turned away.

He shut up the book. Catullus was *also* a fool. That was the only meaning of it. And a whiner, too. Mr. Gibson resolved to be no whiner. He read no more poetry.

His depression did not pass. It deepened. Night and day he lived with it and forgot how it felt to be without it. He began to assume that this was what one got used to, as one grew old.

But a change was coming. The day was coming upon which the women were going, as Mr. Gibson had once put it, into trade. They were going on the same morning, and Mr. Gibson, in his misery, did not bewail the coincidence, for he no longer yearned to be alone with Rosemary.

Ethel, accomplished secretary that she was, had gotten herself a plum of a job that let her off at four in the afternoons. This, she explained with satisfaction, would permit her to be the cook at dinner time.

Rosemary's hours were a little longer. She was going to assist the proprietor of a small dress shop, helping with the stock at first and looking forward to becoming a saleslady. It was an excellent beginning.

In further coincidence, the same day would see the last of Mrs. Violette. Mr. Gibson was going to be alone.

On the eve of this day, the three of them sat in the living room according to habit. Music was playing low from the radio for a cultural background. Rosemary was basting white collar and cuffs upon a navy-blue dress against tomorrow. Ethel was knitting, a thing she did with uncanny skill. (Hours and hours she had sat knitting before her radio, listening to music, to political speeches, to educational programs. She preferred a radio to a record player. She'd never had a record player.) Mr. Gibson was turning the pages of a book sometimes two at a time. His face was calm and benign. The scene was domestic and harmonious, but his sense of it was not . . . for this was the end of his experiment. And now all fell to dust. Rosemary was not only well, she was about to go forth and earn. She needed nothing he could give her, but much that he could not. So now he would let her go . . . he agreed in his heart . . . the sooner the better.

Imagination had painted his future before him. He could see himself and his sister Ethel, mutually helpful and devoted, in some smallish apartment near the college, at work by day until they faltered, and every evening

.thel knitting, the radio on. He said to himself that he
.ould make-do. He had done with much less than a de-
.oted sister at his side. He really did not know why he
.hould feel so disheartened, so desperately unhappy about
.t.

"It all ought to work out very nicely," said Ethel, "although I do dread the bus ride. To be at the mercy of
those buses, thirty minutes each way. A waste, really.
Mightn't it be wise to move a little nearer in to town?"

Rosemary's hands and head jerked. "Move?" she murmured.

"After all," said Ethel, "this *is* pleasant of course, but
when you are working, Rosemary, you won't have the daylight hours . . . Did you prick your finger, dear?"

Rosemary said quietly, "No, Ethel. I did not."

"Ah . . . well." Ethel smiled indulgently. "We ought to
think of Ken, too. Will it be wise for him to ride the buses
in the fall—with that leg?"

"I hadn't thought . . ." said Rosemary in a rush, and
her face came up.

"I should think I could ride on a bus," said Mr. Gibson, "without . . ." His voice caught, because he could
see very plainly the red smear of Rosemary's blood on the
white of the collar in her hands.

"You did run that needle into your finger, dear," said
Ethel chidingly. "Just look at the stain. On your business
clothes, too . . ."

"It will wash," said Rosemary faintly, and rose, and,
walking stiffly, she bore her work toward the kitchen.

Mr. Gibson wondered what it meant. "I suppose," he
said, staring at the cold grate and feeling frozen, "she
pricked her finger and stained the collar because she doesn't
want to go to business tomorrow."

He waited timidly for Ethel to agree.

But Ethel smiled. "I don't think so," she said, "for why
should she tell a lie about that?" (Mr. Gibson faced it.
Rosemary had lied.) "It happened, of course," said Ethel
lowering her voice, "when I spoke of leaving *here*."

"Leaving—?"

"Leaving *him*, I imagine," said Ethel, sotto. "How she
gives herself away!"

He heard her sigh, but inside himself he was collapsing
and shrinking with distaste. Given that nothing is what it
seems; even so, he couldn't guess what it really was. In

the old poems, man was captain of his soul, and he, so steeped in them, would never learn. How could he learn? He was old. His heart sank. Mr. Gibson felt solid, felt treason, too—he couldn't help it—and he hated it. He turned his eyes back into the book and did not look up as Rosemary returned.

"Did you use cold water?" Ethel fussed.

"Of course," said Rosemary softly. "It's nothing." She was taking up her needle, as Mr. Gibson could see through his temple somehow out of the side of his averted face. Did Rosemary know why she had run a needle into her flesh? It made him sad to think, Not necessarily.

"Now, Ken, you will be all right tomorrow?" his sister asked fussily. "Mrs. Violette will be in to finish up your shirts, you know, and she *could* stay and fix your lunch."

"No, no," he said. He didn't want Mrs. Violette. He looked forward to being alone.

"You do feel all right?" said Rosemary timidly anxious. "Nothing's bothering you, Kenneth, is it? You don't look as well as you did, somehow. Do you think so, Ethel?"

"I wonder if I'm not missing my work," he said resettling his shoulders. "I'm used to working . . ."

Rosemary's head bent over her sewing. He wrenched his gaze from her hair.

"You mustn't give me a thought," he said. "In the first place, I have lived alone a matter of nearly half a century, in my day . . . and secondly, the Townsends are right next door, and Paul is around." He despised himself for throwing out Paul's name.

"That's so," said Ethel. "Their new cleaning woman won't be in 'til Friday, and of course Mrs. Violette will be gone. Paul, unless he can shift the load onto Jeanie, is going to be stuck right here with old Mrs. Pyne." She seemed to take a faint malicious satisfaction from this.

"Paul is very good to the old lady," said Mr. Gibson (for jealousy he *would* not descend to, generous and just he *would* be). "I think it's extraordinary."

Rosemary looked up with a flashing smile. "I think so too," she said warmly.

Mr. Gibson turned a page, which was ridiculous. He had not even *seemed* to read it.

"I've wondered," said Ethel with that shrewd little frown of hers. "Are you sure that this property isn't Mrs. Pyne's property? I suppose Paul is her heir."

Rosemary said, smiling, "Sometimes you sound terribly
ynical, Ethel."

"Not at all. I am only a realist," said Ethel smugly. "At
ast I like to think I can face a fact."

"But can't a man be simply good and kind?" Rosemary
iquired. *"Really?"*

Mr. Gibson's heart seemed to swoon.

"And also good-looking?" said Ethel with a grin. "I sup-
ose it's possible. Perhaps he *is* as good as he is beautiful."
he cocked her head and counted stitches.

"But Paul has a prosperous business, hasn't he, Ken-
eth?" insisted Rosemary. "He makes money."

"He is a chemical engineer," said Mr. Gibson. "Yes
. ." (All of a sudden he saw Paul's laboratory like a
vision before him and a row of bottles in a cupboard.
The vision flickered and went away.)

"So he doesn't *need* Mrs. Pyne's money—if she has
any," said Rosemary. "I just don't think he's mercenary."

"Nor do I," said Mr. Gibson, valiantly.

Ethel said, "Of course he isn't, as far as he knows.
Lots of people never admit the most basic facts. However, almost everyone will do an awful lot for material
advantage. . . . Oh, we can kid ourselves, can't we, that
it's for some fancy other reason. But whether you eat,
whether you're comfortable, whether you feel secure,
counts. Indeed it does. And all the time."

"I suppose it does," said Rosemary flushing. She bent
over her handiwork. She seemed defeated.

Mr. Gibson found himself fearing what might be in her
mind. Rosemary had come to him for material comfort,
for security. . . . Oh, she could not have helped herself—
but she knew this now. And so did he. He had urged it.
He had meant it to be so.

"Naturally it counts," he said aloud gently. "Quite naturally so. . . ." He turned a page.

Ethel said with a little snort, "What do you think
a baby yells for? He yells to be warm and fed, and *that is
all*. Let me turn to the weather. I wonder if it will be hot
tomorrow."

Mr. Gibson thought to himself. To be warm. To be
fed, for *me* to be comfortable. . . . Is that what's in the
iceberg? All of our icebergs? Do none of us know *why*
we do anything? Because we won't admit that we are
animals? Ah, but what are we here for, then? Are we

compelled, always, and every time? In all this fluid busy-
ness, has each of us his private doom?

He disliked the idea. He tried to face it. Ethel faced
it. *She* was strong enough. He wouldn't hide from a fact
either . . . not any more. Was it *this* fact that depressed
him so? He seized upon it.

On the air they were talking about a bomb test, with
pious hope that the terrible power would never be un-
leashed against fellow men.

Ethel listened and Ethel said, "Of course they'll un-
leash it."

"The bomb?" Rosemary was startled.

"Do you think they won't?"

"I . . . hope they won't," said Rosemary with wide
eyes.

Ethel shook her graying head. "Be sure they will."

"How can you . . . ?" Rosemary gasped.

"It's just a question of noticing," said Ethel, "that human beings *are* what they *are*. And believe me, a weapon
in the hand is as good as thrown. Don't you know—in cold
fact—that *anything* could cause it to fall? Human beings
are so primitive . . . essentially. They don't mean to be.
You can't call it their fault, but their nature. For which
none of us are to blame. But they get angry; once angry,
they begin to call the other side a monster. There seems
no reason why it is not fine and honorable and brave and
good to slaughter a monster. They do *not* wait and try to
understand or to reason differences away. They simply do
not. And even if they were to try—human reason is so
pitifully new and such a minor factor. . . . People will
always *act* from the blood and the animal residue."

"How do you face a fact like that?" asked Mr. Gibson
quietly.

"The bomb falling?" she said, misunderstanding. "As
far as I am concerned, I'll stay put and be blown up
with the world I know. I don't even want to survive.
Don't tell me you do!" She looked as if he could not possibly be so childish, could he?

"No," said Mr. Gibson thoughtfully. "No . . . not
especially. But then, I am old."

Doom, he thought. Well, then, we are doomed. He
wasn't thinking about the bomb.

"I don't see," said Rosemary to Ethel, "how you have
the courage to think the way you do."

"Courage," said Ethel, "is about the only useful trait. The best we can do is hang onto our nerves and try to understand.

What good is it to understand, thought Mr. Gibson, if we are doomed anyhow? "Then all our pretty intellectual toys . . ." he said, seeing the words he had lived by go sliding into limbo.

"'Toys' is good," said Ethel appreciatively. "Enjoy your poetry while you may, Ken. When or if anyone survives," she shrugged, "be sure there won't be much time for poetry. Now, it hasn't fallen yet," she nodded as if to reassure them, "and I'd like to live out my allotted time just as you would. We have a built-in wish to survive that operates, this side of catastrophe." She smiled. "So let us hope," she said.

"You have no children," said Rosemary in a low voice.

"Neither have you, and let us thank God," said Ethel.

But Mr. Gibson thought, It is true. We are doomed. And the doom is in the iceberg, the undersea part of it. None of us have ever known why we do what we do. We only have the illusion of knowing, the illusion of choice. We are *really* at the mercy of dark things, unknown propulsions. We are blind dupes. That's what Ethel means by reality. Oh yes, and it is true. Mrs. Violette *had* to break the vase. Paul *must* marry someone. Rosemary *must* fall in love with Paul. And I made a fool of myself. But I *had* to. It wasn't my fault. My choices were all made by the genes I got from my mother. Ethel took more from Pa and so is different . . . but she is clearheaded, she at least can *see*.

My whole life has been an illusion. Everyone's life is an illusion. We are at the mercy of what's unknown and cannot be known either. One day we will blow it all up, knock the earth off its orbit, possibly, as surely as Rosemary will go to Paul, as I will send her. . . .

He sunk his head upon his breast, Paul, who was a widower, a chemist, a Catholic . . . Paul was doomed, too. Doomed to be happy and make Rosemary happy, for a little while, before the world blew up.

While he, Kenneth Gibson, would live with his sister and grow older . . . limp out fifteen or twenty years. *Not so!*

There was one rebellious act he could think of. Just

one. He received a tremendous heartening lift of his spirits. A little spunk—he could escape.

And he could remember the number on the bottle.

He slept a little toward morning. When he woke he knew this was the day. He would be alone.

Chapter XII

THE MORNING was bustle. Rosemary, neat and excited, in the navy frock with the white, went first away.

Mr. Gibson followed her to the door. He was wearing his robe of small-figured silk, and in it, he felt the same small neat and decent man he had ever been. He did not know how white and ill he looked.

"Goodbye," she said. "Oh, please, Kenneth, take care . . . ! You worry me. I almost wish . . ."

"No, no, you must not worry." His eyes devoured her. "Goodbye, Rosemary. You must remember . . . this was what I wanted for you."

"To see me well? she asked, "and able? Is that what you mean?"

He didn't answer. He was looking at her face very carefully, since it would be the last time he would see it. He was so *very* fond of her. She *was* his, in a way.

"Is that *all?*" she said suddenly.

Mr. Gibson tried to remember what he had just said. "By no means," he answered steadily. "I want you to be happy, too." He smiled.

"Yes, well . . . I . . ." Her eyes fled and came back. "What can I do to make *you* happier?" she cried. "I'm so—I love you, Kenneth. You know that, don't you?"

It was odd that in this last moment they seemed closer, as he recognized her old familiar passion of gratitude. "I know," he told her gently, "dear girl. I am as happy as I can be," he said with reassuring accents.

Rosemary shook herself and jerked away. He watched her, so straight, so lithe, so healthy—so youthful—down the drive.

Paul Townsend was on the porch sniffing the morning. He waved, but Rosemary didn't see him there. Mr. Gibson was just as glad.

Her loyal nature would doom her to endure.

Ethel went next. "Ken, when you walk to market, pick up a head of lettuce, too? There's a good man."

"I will," he promised.

"And pay Mrs. Violette off . . ."

"Yes."

"And I'll be back, four-ish . . ."

"Yes, Ethel. Goodbye, dear. Good luck. You have been —perfectly fine."

"Pish tush," said Ethel. "Of course. Well, I'm off."

Mr. Gibson closed the door.

He went into the living room and sat down. Mrs. Violette was ironing. He would not, of course, kill himself until she had gone.

He was a fastidious and thoughtful man. (He could not help it.) There would be no mess about this. Nothing distressing for anyone to clean up. Nothing horrible. He knew where he would go and what he would take. It was quick and surely neat. He would be found lying in full decorum on his bed, in all peace. They would think, for a while, that he slept. The shock would thus be graduated and as gentle as he could make it.

But he must leave a letter. The letter must be just so. It must set everything as free as could be.

His blood felt cold. He must try not to be sentimental. This was a choice he was making, icy and clear. He didn't fear the dying. He tried to look beyond.

He had no insurance to be affected by a suicide. Rosemary would have his few bonds, his bank account. Yes, a letter to that effect, too. She'd be all right. Paul would stand by. (She would be free.) Ethel of course was self-sufficient. Ethel would help Rosemary to understand— what he chose they should understand. There was absolutely nothing to worry about.

Except the bomb which would blow up their world one day, but this he could not help.

Everyone's doom was his own.

Mr. Gibson sat in a dream.

At twelve o'clock he was dressed and ready to go downtown, and Mrs. Violette was finished. So he paid her.

"Mr. Gibson, could I have this old string?" she asked

him, and showed him what she had fished from the kitchen wastebasket.

"Of course," he said. "Do you need any more?"

"I got a lot of stuff to tie up," she admitted. "We're going to take 'most everything in the back of the truck."

"How about this?" He gave her a ball of mustard-colored twine.

"That's *Miss* Gibson's." Mrs. Violette's small but ripe-lipped mouth made a hiss of the appellation.

"Well?" he bridled. "Surely I may present you with a bit of string."

Mrs. Violette said, "I don't like to take *her* stuff. Never mind, anyhow. I got to go to the bank and I can pick some up . . ."

"Take it," he said urgently. "I'd like you to take this."

"Well, then . . ." Mrs. Violette seemed to understand his need. She began to wind twine upon her spread fingers.

"No, take it all," he said. "Please do."

"I don't like to take more than I'll use."

"I know that," he told her. This was, he fancied, a rather silly, very trivial rebellion. He just wanted something to be as it used to be. He wanted to feel—generous. (Or . . . for all he knew, he wanted, in some ridiculous revenge, to do his sister Ethel out of the price of a ball of twine.)

Mrs. Violette took the whole ball. "I'm sorry to leave you and Mrs. Gibson," said she.

"I'm sorry if my sister has upset you," he said tiredly.

"Me and Joe are going up to the mountains," said Mrs. Violette. He perceived that this was an answer. "And I got to be ready by five o'clock . . ." She stopped speaking and looked at him. He had the strange conviction that she knew what he proposed to do.

"That's all right," he said soothingly.

Mrs. Violette's face lit in a rare smile. "Well, then, goodbye," she said. "They say that means 'God be with you.' "

"Goodbye," said Mr. Gibson rather fondly.

She went out the kitchen door with the ball of twine in her pocket. Now he was all alone.

At 12:10 o'clock he left the cottage and walked . . . doing quite well without his cane, although he lurched when he came down upon the shortened leg and could not help it . . . went two blocks west, crossed the boulevard there and caught a bus for downtown. Paul Townsend he had left safe at home behind him, working away in his herb garden this morning. So Mr. Gibson knew how to get what he wanted.

He did not see the people on the bus. He did not notice the familiar scenery as the vehicle proceeded on the boulevard, then went threading around residential corners until it came upon a business street and thicker traffic. Mr. Gibson, in a mood both bitter and dangerously sweet, was composing a letter.

There was a temptation to be pathetic, and he must resist it. He must make Rosemary understand the cold choice. He must in no way seem to reproach her . . . A difficult letter. What words would do *this?*

He came out of his absorption in time to get off the bus on a downtown corner. This little city had grown, like all California towns, as a wild weed grows. It had left the college here, and in its own park, close to the town's old center . . . and had sent tentacles romping out into valleys and lowlands on all sides. But Mr. Gibson would not go there, to the college—to walk on a campus path and be spoken to by name . . . not again. They would not miss him very much, he thought. Some younger man would come in. . . .

Paul Townsend's place of business was a block and a half in the opposite direction, and Mr. Gibson turned his uneven steps that way. He began to imagine his next moves . . . and, as he did so, he realized that he ought to have brought a container. He stopped in at a delicatessen and purchased the first small bottle he saw on the shelf. It happened to be a two-ounce bottle of imported olive oil, and quite expensive.

"I am Kenneth Gibson. Mr. Townsend's neighbor. He asked me to stop by and fetch a letter out of his desk," said Mr. Gibson with cool nerves.

"Oh yes. Can I get it for you, Mr. Gibson?"

"He told me exactly where to put my hand on it . . . if you don't mind . . ."

"Not at all," the girl said. "This way, Mr. Gibson." She knew who he was . . . Mr. Gibson of the English Department . . . a trustworthy man. "In here," she said with a smile, and ushered him into the laboratory.

He did not look at the cupboards but went to Paul's desk and opened the left top drawer and took, at random, an old letter out of a pile. "This seems to be the one."

"Good," she said.

"Er . . ." Mr. Gibson looked distressed and embarrassed. "Is there by any chance a . . . er . . . men's room . . .?"

"Oh yes," she said becoming at once crisp and remote. "Right over there, sir." She indicated a door.

"Thank you."

As he had calculated, she left for the outer regions.

He went into the small washroom and turned the cap upon the bottle of olive oil and gravely poured the contents away into the sink.

He came out. Now the laboratory was his alone. He found the key with no trouble. He took down No. 333. His hands were steady as he poured its liquid content into his own container. It was a delicate task, from one small opening into another, but he was cold and clearheaded. He scarcely spilled a drop.

He did not take it all. As he put No. 333 back in place he thought the depletion of the supply would not be noticed for some time. He made no attempt to wipe off fingerprints or anything of that sort. He had elected not to take the whole bottle from the cupboard away with him, only because he needed time. Time to get home. Time to write his letter. He did not want the fact of some missing poison noted too soon and the girl asked and his name given and he interrupted.

Mr. Gibson put the poison he had stolen into the green paper bag, relocked the cupboard, hid the key, left the premises. He thought he might have made a cool and successful thief: he might as well have been a thief all his life for all the difference. . . .

He stood on the downtown corner, waiting for a bus, feeling absolutely numb for the moment. Just as one came, just as he got on, he thought he heard his name spoken. But he wasn't certain, didn't really care whether anyone had called his name or not. . . . so he moved on and sat down by a window.

> I have a tree, a graft of love
> That in my heart has taken root
> Sad are the buds and blooms thereof
> And bitter sorrow is its fruit—

Oh, stop! Stop this senseless jingling of old words. Villon was long dead.

Looking blindly out, the thought crossed his veering mind capriciously that perhaps he'd had, just now, a supernatural warning. But he knew what he was doing. Death. Well? He was simply going to step out of his doom. To him it seemed not an unintelligent thing to do. A *just* God would understand.

How could he put this in a letter? ". . . Very tired . . ." he would write. No. No. It was possible that he would have to lie. What matter if he did or did not lie? ". . . I am not as well as I appear. I have known for a long time . . ." Should he hint that he had begun to doubt his sanity? Yes, *that* . . . Rosemary should understand. And perhaps he *was* insane. In fact, he did not and could not know himself, *really,* why he was doing this deed. Not even this could he know. Doom. In the iceberg of his subconscious the motive lay and worked.

Mr. Gibson, sunk in icy gloom, saw nothing out the windows, nothing inside the bus which went its doomed way on the streets of the town carrying all the doomed people. If he could have done anything for Rosemary, or for any living soul . . . he might have stayed. But all, all were doomed, and to help each other or even to love each other was only another illusion.

Some sense of time and space prodded him to notice the stop that would let him off at the corner where the market was. So he got up and, filled with such pain that he was nearly blinded, he went toward the door. As he stepped off, he thought he heard his name called again.

Angels? Well, if he was about to damn himself through eternity, then he was going to do so. All his life he had done all the duty he had been given to see, made his apparent choices, and if he still had an illusion of choice, this deed appeared to him to be as much his duty as his pleasure . . . and he would do it.

And one duty besides . . . a promise to keep . . . the marketing he had said he would do for Ethel. *Then* he would come (with what relief) to the end of his duties.

So Mr. Gibson went into the big market and took a wheeled basket and pushed it along the aisles. He selected lettuce, he took cocoa, he took a loaf of thin-sliced white bread . . . he took cheese (the kind Ethel preferred). And he took tea for Rosemary. (It might comfort her.)

He stood at the check stand, dumb and lost in utter helplessness, while the girl fingered the buttons and rang the prices. He lifted the big brown bag in his arms. He walked two blocks east, and one north. . . .

The roses at the far side of the cottage were not blooming now.

Old Mrs. Pyne was sitting in her wheel chair on the Townsend's porch. She waved cheerily at him.

Mr. Gibson staggered his course to bring himself near enough to speak to her. (He could ask her. He could inquire about Paul and what the Church might say about marriage and divorcées. . . . But why? He didn't *want* to divorce Rosemary and be, for God knew how many years, her and her husband's friend. No, he didn't *want* that loophole into life. He would rather pretend it wasn't there. Kid himself, he thought bitterly, that the deed would be done for Rosemary's sake.)

He said, "Hello . . ." weakly.

"Goodness!" said the old lady leaning forward, "isn't that too heavy for you, Mr. Gibson?"

"Not too heavy." (But it was. It *was* heavy, his bag of food and death.) "How are you, Mrs. Pyne?" He smiled falsely.

"I'm all right," she said. "Isn't this a glorious day?" Her voice took on a special and almost shocking vigor. "It's so marvelous to be able to sit out in the sun."

"Yes," he said. "Yes . . . well . . ."

He stumbled across the double driveways. He heard Paul's voice calling, "Hi! How goes it?" Mr. Gibson pretended not to hear.

Marvelous to be able to sit in the sun? It was! Yes, it was! He unlocked his door and went in, beginning to know that, quite possibly, he could not do what he had planned to do. So in a night and a morning of acute depression— he had only made a fool of himself once more. He, Kenneth Gibson, was not cut out to be a suicide. No. *He* was fated to set Rosemary free and be her and her husband's good friend for his natural life and limp on in time and bear all. It was not his doom to die today. He couldn't change his doom. Doom is not doom if there is any way out of it. *And he was doomed* . . . to go on being the neat, decent, too thin-skinned little man he had been born to be.

Because it was marvelous to be able to sit in the sun! And this was enough to keep a man alive!

Mr. Gibson began to feel a bit hysterical. No, no, he *would* do it! One second of resolution—that was all he needed. Surely he could manage to lift hand to mouth—one quick gesture—without thought . . .

But if he waited to write a letter. No, no! His whole decision was running away, running out of him. But couldn't the doomed of God ask a little kindness of the devil? Quick, then! Or suffer the tragicomedy out, be a spectator in his own skull and watch his own acts with what bitter amusement could be salvaged.

He was in the kitchen. He did not have—he did not even want—that kind of courage. Not any more.

He put the big brown bag on the counter. He took out the head of lettuce, the piece of cheese, loaf of bread, the box of tea, and, heavy at the bottom of the bag, the can of cocoa. And now he groped for the bottle of death. He would do it *at once!*

The big bag was absolutely empty.

Yes, quickly.

His hand met nothing.

His death would be a mystery: death always was. Where—?

But surely he had put the small *green* paper bag, twisted up around the little bottle, into the market basket, and the checker girl would have put it in with his purchases. She hadn't. It wasn't here.

Where was it? The terrible quick poison he had gone so far to steal?

He searched his jacket pockets. *Not there!*

Had he dreamed the whole thing? No, surely he remembered pouring the olive oil into the sink far too vividly to have done it in a dream. He had lost it? But the poison was *now* in a bottle labeled "olive oil." Nobody would have any way of knowing it *was* poison! Colorless, odorless, instant . . .

What had he done?

Oh, what wicked error had he made this time?

Where had he left a bottle of poison that looked so innocent? In what public place where innocent people came and went?

The shock nearly caused him to fall down. Then his blood raced and cried *no no no* in perfect revulsion.

Well, it was the end of him. The end of Kenneth Gibson. The end of all respect for him, forever. But *somebody else* was going to get the poison and die of it unless he could prevent this.

The lightning change of all his purposes sent him stumbling to the telephone. He dialed. He said, "Police." His voice did not sound like his own. Every bit of any kind of courage he had, stiffened his spine. Face it. All right. *No nonsense, now.* A sickness seemed to fall off him.

The front door of the cottage opened. His wife Rosemary was standing there.

"I came," she said, intent upon herself and her own thoughts, "because I have got to talk to you. I can't—be such a rabbit—" Her face changed. "Kenneth, what's the matter?"

He had held up his hand for her to be silent. He thrust away every thought but one.

"Police? This is Kenneth Gibson. I have mislaid a small bottle filled with deadly poison." He articulated very clearly and spoke forcefully. "The bottle is labeled olive oil. It is roughly a pyramid, about five inches high, and it's inside a green paper bag. Nobody is going to know that it is poison. Can you do anything? Can you find it? Can you put out a warning?"

Rosemary shrank back against the door.

"I stole it. From a laboratory. . . . Can't give you the name of the stuff. It is odorless, tasteless . . . fatal. . . . Yes, sir. I took a Number Five bus at the corner of Main and Cabrillo at about a quarter after one o'clock. Got off at Lambert and the Boulevard . . . must have been one forty-five. I was in the market there possibly ten or fifteen minutes. It's just after two o'clock now. . . . Yes. Walked to my house . . . and just now discovered I haven't got it. . . . No, I am absolutely sure. . . . *I* put it in the olive-oil bottle. . . . Brand? King somebody-or-other. . . . Yes, I did that. . . . Why? Because I was going to use it myself," he told the barking questioner on the line. "I intended to kill myself."

Rosemary whimpered. He did not look at her.

"Yes, I know it may kill somebody else. That's why I'm calling. . . ." The voice raged in a controlled way. "Yes, I am criminal," said Mr. Gibson. "Anything you say. Find it. Please, do all you can to find it."

He gave his name again. His address. His phone number.

He put the phone upon the cradle.

"Why?" said Rosemary.

He had thought never to see her again.

"Kenneth, I didn't. I didn't. Forgive me. I *didn't—*"

He scarcely heard what she said. He spoke harshly. "Go back to your shop. Know nothing about this. Don't get into it. Leave me. I may have caused someone to die. I may be a murderer. No good to you now. Leave me." He willed her to vanish.

Rosemary shoved herself away from the slab of the door, and stood on her feet. She said, "No. I will not leave you. It isn't going to happen. Nobody will be poisoned. We will go and find it."

He made a gesture of despair. "Oh no, mouse, no use to dream . . ."

"That's *wrong*," said Rosemary. *"That's untrue.* We *can* find the poison. *I* can— and *I will.* And you'll come too. Paul will help us!" she cried and whirled and opened the door. "Come . . ." she said imperiously.

"All right," said Mr. Gibson. "We can try, I suppose."

He walked out into the sunshine. He was very cold. He was as good as dead. He was so ruined a man by this stroke of fate or whatever it was—it seemed to him that he had most unfortunately survived himself.

Rosemary ran, calling, "Paul! Paul!"

Paul bobbed up from behind a hedge. "What's up?" he said cheerfully.

"Help us. Kenneth had some poison. . . . He's left it someplace. We have to find it."

"Poison! What's this!"

"Your car. Please. *Please,* Paul. It's in a bottle labeled olive oil. Anybody might get it. He's left it at the market. Or on a bus. We have to go there."

Paul tossed her some keys. "Get out the car," he said. His hand clenched around Mr. Gibson's forearm. "What's she talking . . . ?"

"It is Number Three thirty-three," Mr. Gibson said perfectly distinctly, "I went downtown and stole it from your cupboard."

"What in *hell—!*"

"I was going to kill myself," said Mr. Gibson without apology. "Now I may kill somebody else."

Paul stepped back and withdrew his hand as if from contamination. He turned and yelled at Rosemary. "Did you call the police?"

She was vanishing into Paul's garage. "Yes! Yes! Hurry! Hurry!" she shouted.

Paul said, "Got to tell Mama—get a shirt—" He leaped up on his porch. "Don't go without me," he yelled back over his shoulder. Mr. Gibson stood still. Rosemary was in the garage trying to start a strange car.

But the quiet neighborhood was still quiet. This crisis was like a dagger plunged into flesh that did not yet feel any wound. He, the cause, stood still and could smell lavender and feel the weight of the sun's heat. He experienced a moment out of time. He might as well have killed himself, for he knew he was lost. But also he was being born again. He closed his eyes and turned his face to the caress of the light.

Then Paul's De Soto came bucking and plunging backward. It stopped and Rosemary swung the door and leaned out. "Get in."

Mr. Gibson went meekly, and climbed into the front seat as she shoved over. She seemed to be quite sure that Paul was coming to do the driving.

Paul came in an instant, buttoning a blue shirt over his naked chest. He shoved long legs under the wheel. "Where to, Rosie?"

"The market," she said decisively.

Mr. Gibson sat in the middle. He might as well have been a wax dummy.

"I called Jeanie to come home," Paul said, speaking as if his teeth were ready to chatter. "She's at her music lesson. Mama will be all right alone for half an hour. I'd just helped her to lie down. Didn't tell *her* why. Couldn't leave her with a shock. . . . What got into him?" said Paul angrily.

"I must have been crazy," said Mr. Gibson quietly. It was the easiest thing to say. He was beyond horror and beyond pain.

"Pray it's in the market," said Rosemary, "and they've found it. Paul, do you know what it is? It *is* poison?"

"It's dangerous stuff, all right. As I told him—How did he get *at* it?" Paul demanded with that anger.

The ghost of Mr. Gibson explained, and Paul grimaced as if he had to hold his teeth clenched. There seemed a convention that Mr. Gibson could speak and be heard and yet not be considered quite solidly there. Paul was perspiring. The car went jerkily. It was only three blocks to the market. "What are you doing home, Rosie?" Paul said in a nervous explosion.

"I wanted to talk to him. Alone. I didn't *like*— This is the first day Ethel's been . . ." They had turned the corner "Look! A police car!"

If Mr. Gibson felt a twinge: it felt like simple wonder. What, he wondered, was going to happen next?

He tried to push at this wonder and make himself feel alive. What was he doing plunging around the streets—? Who was he? Who were these people, young, busy, pushing people . . . Rosemary thrusting both legs out of the car to the pavement of the market's oarking lot and Paul yanking on the brake and tumbling out the other side.

Mr. Gibson sat for a moment, abandoned and strangely exposed, for both front doors of Paul's car were flapping open. When he felt a stirring somewhere at the bottom of his being it was still remarkably simple. It was curiosity.

So he slid under the wheel and got, as nimbly as he could, out of the car. He limped rapidly after them into the market.

Chapter XIII

SURE I know him," The little checker girl was saying. She had black tangled hair, enormous dark eyes, and wore huge gold buttons in her ears. "I always thought he was *nice*, you know what I mean? Sure, I saw him. *That's* him, isn't it? But I didn't see no green paper bag. It *wasn't* in with his groceries. He didn't *have* no green paper bag. See . . ." She moved closer to the tall policeman and looked up at him almost yearningly. "We aren't busy so close to lunch. We never are. So I seen him come in. Right in that door. He didn't look good. He looked like he was sick or something. I seen his bare hands. If he had it, then he musta had it in his pocket. Did you look in his pockets?"

"Did you look in your pockets?" Rosemary flashed around and seemed to bear down upon him. (She wasn't anybody he knew.' Then the policeman seemed to be searching him while Mr. Gibson stood helpless as a dummy or a small child whose elders don't trust the accuracy of his reports.

The checker girl said, almost weeping, "Why'd he want to do a thing like that? Gee, I thought he was *nice*. . . . I mean some customers aren't so nice, you know, but *he* was nice." She used the past tense as if he had died. Nobody answered her.

"And listen," she sobbed. "I didn't put no green paper bag in with anybody else's stuff, either. Only been three or four people through my stand. It isn't *here*. Probably he never had no poison.' She peeked at Mr. Gibson fearfully.

"If it isn't here,' said Rosemary, tensely, "it must be on the bus."

"Wa-ait a minute," the policeman said. "Now—" His eyes were cold. They fixed upon Mr. Gibson as if he were an object and an obstacle. 'One could tell that he was used to obstacles.' "You are positive that you had this green paper bag with this poison in it when you got on the bus?"

"Yes, I am positive," said Mr. Gibson with perfect composure.

"And when you got home?"

"It wasn't there."

"You were emotionally upset?" the policeman said. "You think you forgot it on the bus, then?"

"I 'forgot' it," said Mr. Gibson, "because, I suppose, subconsciously I did not really want . . ." The words were coming out of him as from a parrot.

Rosemary took his arm rather roughly. "Do you *want* a stranger to die?" she cried at him.

The knife went in. "No," said he. "No. No."

"Well, then!' said Rosemary with a curious air of triumph. "You see, it *isn't* true!"

Paul said, "Wait a minute. What are the police doing?"

The policeman said. "They are after the bus, all right. And we are broadcasting. I'll search this building thoroughly, now, just in case . . ."

"What do you think the chances . . . ?"

The policeman shrugged. He didn't think much of them. He was a sad man. He'd seen a lot of trouble. He did his best and let it go at that. "Whoever might find a bottle—looks like it's olive oil—might throw it away," said he. "Might take it home—use it. Who can say what people are going to do?"

Ethel can, thought Mr. Gibson, and for a moment feared he might whinny this forth nervously.

"Can't *we* find the bus?" Rosemary was urging.

"Gee, Rosie, I dunno," said Paul. "Are you sure he shouldn't be seeing a doctor . . ." Paul jittered.

Rosemary said, "Hurry, hurry . . ."

The checker girl said, "Oh gosh, I hope you find it! I hope nothing bad is going to happen!" She peered at Mr. Gibson from her eye corners. "Look, you're all right now, aren't you?" She seemed to care.

Mr. Gibson couldn't answer. What was it to be "all right," he wondered, with a shadowy sadness.

Then they were back in the car, as before.

"Number Five. That is the bus that goes on out the boulevard?" asked Rosemary.

"Yes."

"But how will we know which one? Did you notice any number on it?"

"No."

"But the police could get the number of the right bus, couldn't they? Since they know the time you caught it downtown, the time you got off at the market."

"Maybe."

"Then, maybe they have caught it already. They *must* have. It's two fifteen."

Rosemary was babbling! It was vocalized worry. Mr. Gibson was answering in monosyllables. Paul was driving the car. He wasn't driving it very well. The car jerked and jittered. The man was nervous. Mr. Gibson—so curiously removed from self by his ruination (which was complete) —found his senses able to perceive. He felt a resurgence of an old power. He was no longer cut off. Paul, he realized, shrank from him as evil. Paul was almost superstitiously afraid of a man who had intended to kill himself.

Mr. Gibson wondered if he ought to try to explain. The trouble was . . . he could not now remember how it had gone, all his reasoning. He thought it odd to be sitting in the middle with the two of them so bent on preserving him from the doom of becoming a murderer. Doom . . . ah yes, that was the word. Now he remembered. . . .

"I was going to write a letter," he said out loud. "I was going to explain . . . At least, I—"

"Well, *don't!*" said Rosemary vehemently. "Not now. Just don't *talk* about it. Whatever you thought, whatever it was, whatever it *is*. Now, we have to find that terrible stuff and stop it from hurting anyone. Afterward," she said grimly, "you can talk about it if you want to. Paul, can you drive faster?"

"Listen," said Paul, nervous and sweating. "I'd just as soon not wreck us, you know . . ."

Rosemary said, "I know. I know," and she pounded with her small female fists the side of Paul's car. "But I *am* to blame for *this*," said Rosemary.

Mr. Gibson tried to protest but she turned and looked fiercely into his eyes. "And *you* are to blame. *We* are to blame. That has to be true. I'll prove it to you. I'm tired," she cried. "I am so tired—"

Paul said, "Don't talk, Rosie. He must have been crazy. Let it go and say he was crazy."

But Mr. Gibson had a strange feeling of solidity. He thought, Yes, of course, I am to blame.

The boulevard was a divided street. In the weedy center space there lay old streetcar tracks, now superseded by the bus line. The boulevard was lined with little low apartment buildings, arranged in the charming California style, around grassy courts, and in a gay variety of colors . . . pink ones, yellow ones, green ones . . . all sparkling clean and bright in the light of this fine day. Like big beads on the pretty chain, there came from time to time the shopping centers. A huge food market, with banks of red and yellow and orange fruit along the sidewalk, its bulk like a mother hen beside its chicks—the drugstore, laundromats.

After ten minutes of going, the boulevard lost its center strip and became just a street curving off through residential patches into a long valley, where houses became smaller and shabbier and more countrified as the city frayed about the edges. Mr. Gibson, sitting in the middle, looked at all this scenery as if he had come upon a new planet.

They passed one bus going their way, and, after a while, another. Neither could be the right one.

It was Paul Townsend, now, who was doing the talking. "Number Five turns around at the junction, I think. Let's see. If you got off about one forty-five, then *it* would get to the end of its line around two forty or a bit after. We might meet the right bus, coming *back*. What is it now? Two thirty."

"I can't tell the right bus," Mr. Gibson said.

"The police can. Watch the other side of the street . . ."

Mr. Gibson's brain, although feebly, was turning over. "Whoever found the bottle," said he with detached composure, "may have gotten off the bus at any stop along the way."

"Yes, but—" Paul's eye flirted nervously toward him. Paul wanted to worry out loud, but not this much.

"In fact, once the bus has turned around to come back —that means that every person who was on it while *I* was on it, *must not* be on it any more."

"Maybe whoever found it turned it over to the driver. Maybe they have like a lost and found department . . ."

"Maybe," said Mr. Gibson stoically.

"Who's going to take and eat food that he just *found?*" said Paul. "Especially if it looks as if it has been opened. Did you break a seal?"

"No seal. It was a question of turning the cap . . ."

"How full was the bottle?"

"Full enough."

"It wouldn't pour quite like olive oil."

"It's oily enough," said Mr. Gibson. "The bottle will smell of olive oil."

"Listen—" said Paul, "even if we don't find it . . . don't forget the police are putting the alarm on the air. That's what he said."

"Not everyone," said Mr. Gibson, "listens constantly to the radio."

Rosemary said, "And we should face the facts, shouldn't we?" She turned her head and looked fiercely at him as before. Her eyes were such a fierce blue. Mr. Gibson realized that inside the body of Rosemary—behind the face of Rosemary—within all the graces of Rosemary, which graces he loved— there was somebody else. A fierce angry determined spirit he had never met and never known. This spirit said boldly, "If anyone dies of that poison, you'll go to jail, I suppose?"

"I suppose," he said and felt indifferent.

"In any case, you'll lose your position?"

"Yes."

"People will know . . ."

The people in the market, the people on the bus, the police, the neighbors, the public. Yes, thought Mr. Gibson, everyone will know. . . .

"But if nobody dies and we find the poison," said Rosemary, *"everything else we can bear.* Isn't that a *fact?"*

Mr. Gibson put his hand up to shield his eyes. It *was* a fact, as far as he could tell.

"Keep your chin up," said Paul nervously. "Who knows? What time is it? Ten of three—the bus has turned around."

"Look!" said Rosemary. "Look . . . up ahead! There it is! There it is!"

Chapter XIV

THERE WERE in fact, two buses. One wide yellow vehicle was pulled up on the shoulder of the road. A black-and-white police car nosed against it from behind. Beside it stood a group of three, two policemen and the bus driver.

The other bus had stopped a few yards ahead and a group of people—ten or a dozen—were climbing on. These people seemed, all of them, to be looking back with crooked necks toward the policemen.

Paul made a wild U-turn. His car stuttered and bounced and stopped behind the police car. The time was 2:54. Mr. Gibson found himself limping after his companions over lumpy sod through tall dust-plastered weeds that grew between the road and a patched wire fence. It was an unexpected setting for a crisis. Most crises, thought Mr. Gibson, take place in unexpected settings.

"I'm Mrs. Gibson," he heard Rosemary cry. "It was my husband .   Did you find it? Is it *here?* The poison?"

Not one of the three men opened his mouth. So Mr. Gibson knew that they had not found it.

"Who are those people getting on that other bus?" cried Rosemary against their silence. "What's happening?'

"Passengers," said one of the policeman. "They don't—none of them—know anything. We're letting them go about their business." He swung around. "You the man left this poison someplace in the olive oil bottle?" He had selected

Mr. Gibson instead of Paul . . . and Mr. Gibson nodded.

"Well, we can't find it on this bus."

"Which seat did you sit in?" snapped the second police-man.

Mr. Gibson shook his head.

"How big was the package?"

Mr Gibson showed them mutely, using his hands.

"In a *paper* bag?"

Mr: Gibson nodded. This policeman, a young one, gave him a disgusted look, sucked air into the corner of his mouth, and swung up through the open door of the bus. He didn't like any part of this situation. His partner, an older man, with a thicker mask on, helped Rosemary up by her elbow. Paul went, too. Four of them ducked and bobbed, searching in there, where the policemen must already have searched.

Mr. Gibson stood in the dusty weeds. This was the bus? He had ridden this bus? He had no recollection of any details at all. Now, here he was, standing in the sun, on the dusty earth, with a field spreading away from him . and he, his own survivor.

The bus driver, a lean man in his thirties with a long and rather surprisingly pale face, stood in the weeds, too, hands deep in trouser pockets, watching him. "So you would your own quietus make? Hey?" said the bus driver softly.

Mr. Gibson was immeasurably startled. "I botched it," said he pettishly.

The bus driver poked out his lips and seemed to be touching his tongue up over his teeth. He moved back far enough to lean in at the door of the bus. "This man sat halfway back on the right side, near the window, alone," he bawled.

The four inside responded by gathering together on the right side of the bus. The driver came forward far enough to lean on the high yellow bus wall.

"You botched it, all right," he said to Mr. Gibson. "Hamlet made a mess of it, too. Hey? Going to try again?" He had sandy lashes.

"I doubt it." snapped Mr. Gibson. "I'll take what's coming to me." He pulled back his shoulders.

"Gibson, hey? Teach at the college, don't you?" the man said. "What do you teach?"

"Poetry."

"Poetry! Hah!" The man grinned. "There's a million poems about death, I guess."

"And about love, too." said Mr. Gibson with frozen-feeling lips. This was the oddest, the most unexpected conversation he had ever gotten into.

"Sure—love and death," the bus driver said, "and God and man—and all the real stuff."

"Real?" Mr. Gibson blinked.

"You think it *ain't?*" the bus driver said. "Don't gimme that."

The younger policeman came out of the bus. "Nope," he said. "No soap. We'll look again in a few minutes."

"Yeah?" said the driver. "Whassa matter? Don't you trust yourselves?"

"Eyes can do funny tricks," the policeman said stiffly.

"O.K. by me. I don't mind being out of service. Nice day." The bus driver looked at Mr. Gibson again with contemplative eyes.

Rosemary jumped down out of the bus. "What can we *do?*"

Paul behind her, took her arm. "Better go home, Rosie," he murmured. "The broadcast is the only hope, now. Nothing *we* can do but wait."

"You remember him?" cried Rosemary to the bus driver.

"Sure do, ma'am."

"Did you see the paper bag.'

"Might have," said the bus driver, narrowing his eyes. "Seems to me I get the impression he shifted a little package to his other hand when he put his fare in. It's just an impression but I *got* it. Might mean something."

"Did you see it in his hand when he got off?"

"No, ma'am. People getting off have their backs to me."

"Did you see who took the seat he'd been sitting in . . . ?"

"No, ma'am. Lessee. He got off at Lambert? Well, I had a little poker game with a green Pontiac there—where he got off. This Pontiac and me was outbluffing each other, so I paid no attention. . . ."

"Was the bus full?"

"No, ma'am. Not at that hour."

"Do you *understand?*" said Rosemary. "It's a deadly poison. In the wrong bottle. Do you *understand* that?"

The bus driver said sweetly. "I understand."

"Did you notice *anyone* getting off with a green paper bag?"

"I can't see their hands when they're getting off, ma'am," he reminded her patiently.

Rosemary clasped her own hands and looked off across the field.

Paul said, "Somebody picked it up and took it and there's no way of finding out who. . . . The broadcast warning will either reach him or it won't."

The two cops were listening quietly. The older one shifted his weight.

"Maybe," said Rosemary. "Maybe there *is* something we can do. You were there," she said to the bus driver. "Did you recognize *anybody else* who was on the bus then?"

"Hey?" said the bus driver, wrinkling his brow.

"Anyone else we could find and ask? Somebody who was also there and might have noticed?"

"Wait a minute." The driver seemed to bristle up. "This stuff's poison, hey?"

Paul said, "Damned dangerous," and looked angry. "He took it from my lab. He knew what it was. He should never . . . Oh, come home, Rosie."

"A stranger," said Rosemary, still addressing the bus driver, "trusting in a label. Some stranger to us, who doesn't want to die. People do trust labels. . . ."

"Yes," he said, "they got a right to. And there was my blonde."

"Blonde?"

"Yeah, and while *she* wouldn't . . . I don't *think*. . . . Nobody," said the bus driver forcefully, heaving himself away from his leaning position, "is going to poison my blonde!" He grew taller. "Is that your car?"

"Who is this blonde?" the young policeman said moving in.

"I don't know her name."

"Where does she live?"

"I don't know where she lives."

"She was *on* the bus?"

"Yeh, she was on the bus."

"If you don't know her . . . how come . . . ?"

"She doesn't know that she's my blonde—not yet. One of these days . . . Aw, I was biding my time. Now look," the bus driver said, "I'm *going*. One thing I *do* know and that's the stop she gets off at. *I* can find her. And nobody's going to poison my blonde."

He set off toward Paul's car.

"Oh yes! Paul," Rosemary cried, "Kenneth, come on! We'll all go, find her. *She* might have noticed . . . Hurry, come on!"

The whole group was streaming toward Paul's car.

The older policeman said, "Wait . . . I can call in, you know. I can get a prowl car there in seconds . . ."

"Where?" said the driver. "When I don't know where myself? All I got is the stop. Corner of Allen and the Boulevard. What can *you* do with that? Thanks, anyway, but I guess I got to go find her myself. I'll know her when I see her, see?"

"What about this bus?"

"Life and death," said the driver, with his hand on Paul's car. "Let them fire me." Paul was right behind him. "Give me the keys," the driver said.

"My car . . . I'll drive." Paul looked as if he were suffering. His mouth was grim.

"You are an amateur," said the bus driver, and took the keys out of Paul's hand.

Mr. Gibson knew only that Rosemary's hands were pulling and hustling him. He and she got into the back seat. Paul got in beside the bus driver.

"Good luck," said the older policeman, rather kindly. "Call in, now." The younger one was chewing grass.

The bus driver was moving levers. Paul's car surged backward, slipped out into traffic. It seemed to respond with pleasure to a master's hand. "I can make better time, that's all," the bus driver said. "Driving's my business. Every business has its skills."

"That's all right," Paul murmured.

They were sailing back toward town.

Chapter XV

MY NAME'S LEE COFFEY," said the bus driver suddenly. Paul straightened up with an effect of relaxing, of feeling better. "I'm Paul Townsend," he said in something nearer his normal amiable voice. "A neighbor of the Gibsons'."

"I see. And the lady is Mrs. Gibson."

"Rosie," said Paul, "this is Lee Coffey—"

"Her name is Rosemary," Mr. Gibson heard himself saying loudly. "My name is Kenneth Gibson. I am the man . . ."

"How do, Mrs. Rosemary?" the bus driver said over his shoulder. "Say, Mr. Kenneth Gibson, what *was* it that was coming to you . . . you'd rather take poison?"

Mr. Gibson tried to swallow with a dry mouth.

Paul said quickly, "No, no, don't talk about it. It was a temporary . . . He didn't even know what he was doing. He must have been crazy. He's all right now."

"What puts him all right, all of a sudden?" the bus driver said.

"Why, he knows . . . he has friends. He's got everything to live for."

"Candy?" said the bus driver.

"I don't know what you mean."

"I never could get that," said the bus driver, sliding the car skillfully to a strategic position in the center lane. "How come—now you take a suicide sitting on a ledge up high, see . . . ? People trying to talk him out of it, offer the same as lollypops. Everybody's his friend, they tell him. Come home, the dog needs him. Or he can have beer. He can have chocolate. . . . Seems to me if a man gets to the point of taking his life he's got more serious things in his mind. It's no time for candy, is it?"

"You are wrong," said Mr. Gibson forcefully.

"That so?"

"There is one moment when a lollypop is enough, either way."

"I see," said the bus driver. "Yeah . . . . well, *you'd* know. That's very interesting."

The car moved. It was not speeding. But no second was lost by indecision or by fumbling. Mr. Gibson found himself admiring this with peculiar pleasure.

"If you *want* to talk about it . . ." the bus driver said, and Paul said again, "No, no . . ."

Mr. Gibson answered truthfully. "I'd like to talk to *you* about it. Not just now, I guess." He felt expanded and relaxed in contact with a mind that interested him. A mind that cheerfully pried off a certain lid . . . a lid that had been stifling and muffling and shutting up that which is interesting.

He looked sideways at Rosemary, and her eyes were

visited by the ghost of a smile. "Tell me about your blonde, Mr. Coffey," she said almost brightly.

"Look at me, rushing to the rescue," the bus driver said, "of a blonde who doesn't know she's mine. I'll tell you a little bit. I see her nearly every day. Watch for her, now. I'm getting to know her. I'm thinking of getting up the nerve to speak to her. Never have. Doesn't matter. I already know that I like her a lot. So how can I let her get the poison? Will this offend her, Mrs. Gibson?"

"Rosemary," said Rosemary gravely. "No, it won't offend her, Mr. Coffey. It won't offend her at all."

"Call me Lee," said the bus driver. "These are unusual circumstances. Listen, Rosemary, she is a beautiful blonde."

"You are a very interesting man," said Rosemary.

"That's possible," said Lee Coffey thoughtfully.

It was Paul who came in with an ordinary question. "Have you been a bus driver long?"

"Ten years. Since I got out of the Army. Because I like to think."

"Like to think?" Paul repeated after him, seeming to find this shockingly obscure.

"Ruminate. Ruminate," said the bus driver. "That's why I like a useful but not creative job. You start pushing and trying to a purpose . . . or even just trying to make a million dollars . . . it warps your thinking. *My* thinking, anyhow. The kind I like."

Paul said, impatient with bewilderment, "How can you possibly find this girl, this blonde, whoever she is . . . ?"

"He'll find her," said Rosemary with parted lips. "Don't you think so, Kenneth?"

"I do," said Mr. Gibson. "I think so." He felt astonished. The car slipped up to a red light and stopped smoothly.

"Mr. Coffey—Lee." Suddenly Rosemary took in a great breath and threw herself on her knees in the tonneau. "Please help me? Tell me something?"

"Sure if I can . . ."

"You are an expert driver. I can see that you are. Will you tell me . . . I believe you will *know*. I can believe *you*."

"What's the trouble?" said the bus driver, sending them swiftly off the mark as the light changed.

Mr. Gibson sat astonished while Rosemary knelt and poured out words toward this bus driver's ear.

"It is a foggy night," she said. "I am driving. I am try-ing to be careful. I know . . . to the best of my knowledge . . . that I am on the right side of the road."

"Go ahead," said the bus driver encouragingly.

"I also think I know that there is a deep ditch to my right. I think we have come that far . . . you see?"

"Yeah . . . yeah . . ."

"All of a sudden there is a car coming head on . . . and *he* is on his *left* side of the road. I have to do something quick."

"Can't deny that," said Lee Coffey cheerfully.

"I turned *left*," said Rosemary intensely. "You see, I thought . . ." She buried her head on her arm.

"So what happened?" asked the driver.

"He turned to his right, so we collided. Please tell me. *You* tell me if I was wrong."

The bus driver turned the situation over in his mind. Meanwhile, they glided upon the boulevard, having al-ready reached the spot where the divided street began. The scenery floated by.

"You had three choices," the man said calmly in a mo-ment. "You could turn right, supposed to be proper . . . and take a chance on the ditch. Pretty sure to be dangerous. You could stay where you were because you are legal . . . and take the chance the other fella's going to correct him-self and turn off in time. That takes cold nerve and an awful lot of stubborn righteousness. Or, you can turn left as you did and figure to get around him on the *clear* side . . . even though it's the *wrong* side . . . of the road. Hey?"

"It seemed clear . . ."

"Was it?"

"Well, yes, actually it *was* clear. You see, I thought . . . I thought *he* might be confused and think he was on his right side. I didn't know he'd turn off. How could I know that?'

"You did no wrong," Lee Coffey said gravely. "You tried for a solution. Who can do more? Makes sense to me."

Rosemary's breath shuddered in. "But the result was that the car hit us on our right, and—Kenneth was hurt. . . . *Only* Kenneth was hurt. Not me. Tell me, please . . . did I mean to put him between me and that other car? Did I choose to hurt him rather than myself? Is *that* why I turned to the left, *really?*"

"You just told me why you turned left, didn't you?" Lee Coffey said.

"I thought I was trying to save us both. But, you see . . . there was no ditch. I was mistaken about that. We hadn't come to the place where the ditch began to be there, along the right side of the road."

"Fog," said the bus driver. "O.K. You *were* on the right?"

"Yes."

"He, the other fella, *was* on his left?"

"Yes."

"And you thought there was this ditch?"

"I think I thought—but Ethel—says, there's no such thing as an accident. As if—as if . . . subconsciously I *made* happen what I *wanted* to happen . . ."

"No such thing as an accident!" cried the bus driver. "Where has this Ethel been living?"

"Wait," said Rosemary, warningly. "She's . . . very wise. She's not stupid . . . and she's good . . ."

"She is, eh? Well, I'll tell *you* something. Nobody's that wise. There happen to be plenty of accidents."

"But *are* they? *Really?*"

"The subconscious, hey?" said the bus driver. "Well, I see what she's getting at, all right. Sure. Some people are accident-prone . . . this is a thing that's been discovered. It's like some people take to getting sick because they'd rather . . . Certainly. But not so, in your case."

"Not—?" Rosemary trembled.

"*How* so?" demanded the bus driver. "What did your subsconscious *do?* Explain it to me. Did it go up in the ether someplace and have a conference with the other fella's subconscious? He didn't have any accident either if Ethel is right. Hey? So did your subconscious say to the other subconscious, 'Look here, old chap, I'm fixing to have an accident. Is this O.K. with you? How about right now?" So the other subconscious says, 'Fine, fine. Well met. Me, too. *I* was fixing to have an accident, myself . . . and now is as good a time as any. So here's how we'll work it . . .' Aaah . . ." The bus driver gave an effect of spitting over the side. "Explain to me how these two subconsciouses met, there and then, if not *accidentally?* Or if you're going to say . . . well, only one of them *meant* to do it . . . Now you got to admit the *other one* anyhow had an

accident. So which one of you did . . . or didn't? You or
him? Hey?"

Rosemary said nothing. She knelt as if in prayer.

"Certainly," Coffey continued, "there'd be no accidents
if you could know everything. But who can know everything? You can anticipate just so much. You cannot—
now I don't care—you *cannot* always guess when who is
going to do what, where. Neither you nor your subconscious, either! It's too much! There's too damned much
going *on* in this universe. So there's going to happen what
we call accidents. You see what I mean?"

"Yes," said Rosemary. "Yes, I do." She sighed deep.

"Those who skin out of having accidents are the ones
who take care, who look ahead and so forth. But on top
of that they better have some very snappy reflexes. See?
And even they don't always skin out of all the things they
meet—"

"Rosemary," said Mr. Gibson sternly. "Ethel never said
this thing to you. She couldn't have told you that you
deliberately hurt me."

"Not deliberately. No—but she thinks I *must* have
meant to, because I *did*," Rosemary sobbed. "She keeps
saying she doesn't 'blame' me. She keeps saying she 'understands.' Oh, Kenneth, I'm sorry—I wouldn't say a word
against Ethel but this . . . this has been . . ."

Paul said angrily, "I told you you shouldn't pay any
attention to Ethel."

"Easier said than done," said the bus driver . . . bluntly,
accurately, and astonishingly.

"Doom," murmured Mr. Gibson, recovering from a
stunned sensation. "Yes—doom—well. . . ."

"Now, the subconscious," said the bus driver, throwing out one hand as if he had been lecturing all along and
was starting a new paragraph. "It's down there and it
operates all right, *something* like they say. There's a little
more to it. For instance, *why* would you want to hurt
him?"

"Because—" said Rosemary indistinctly. "But it isn't
true." She wiggled back up upon the seat.

"I'd say you had an accident," Lee Coffey told her.
"For the love of Pete, Mike, and Maria . . . I don't
see the point of this Ethel!"

Rosemary was crying.

Mr. Gibson began to feel quite angry for Rosemary's sake. "Ethel isn't infallible, mouse," he said indignantly. He felt a surge of malicious mischief, too. "I've heard Ethel say, for instance, that bus drivers are perfectly ruthless brutes. Now, obviously . . ."

"What!" Lee Coffey raised his head. "Let me tell you, for your information, *nobody's* got more ruth than us bus drivers. Ruth's our business. It's a job, takes a mighty responsible party and no joking. You got to drive in whatever weather, whatever traffic, and *on* schedule, and what you meet you meet with your mind on safety first. Listen, we got more ruth than any twenty-five private drivers in this world." He was sputtering. "We *can't* take chances. We aren't *free* to. Passengers, pedestrians, school kids, nuts, drunks . . . we got to look out for everybody in the world. We got to handle it, and if we *do* have an accident, believe me, it *is* an accident. What's this Ethel talking? Who *is* this Ethel?"

"My sister," said Mr. Gibson, tossed in the storm of this outburst, yet somehow wanting to laugh out loud, which seemed unsuitable.

"Some sister," said the bus driver gloomily.

"She came to . . . take care of us . . . after the accident . . ."

"I must confess," said Paul, his syllables falling rapidly, "that we don't . . . Mama and Jeanie and I . . . we just don't care too much for Ethel. She seems so cold and superior . . ."

"My sister Ethel!" said Mr. Gibson.

"Ruthless. Hey?" muttered the bus driver. "Every last one of us, hey? The whole category? 'Ay, in the catalogue ye go for men . . .'"

"You are fond of Shakespeare?" asked Mr. Gibson.

"Sure, I am. Not only his language hits the spot: his music does, too. *You* like Shakespeare, don't you?"

"I like Shakespeare very much," said Mr. Gibson with his hair rising on his head in delighted astonishment. "Do you like Browning?" he asked with strange urgency.

"Some of it. Quite a lot of it. Of course you got to get onto his system."

"He was kind of a lady's man."

"The ladies were the ones who had the time to—you know—ruminate, in a refined way," said Lee Coffey, "or

they used to before they started being riveters and ty-
coons."

"Just so," said Mr. Gibson almost comfortably.

Rosemary was not weeping any more. She sat with
her shoulder to his. "Did you ever hear Ethel speak of a
blonde?" she said demurely.

"What'd she say?" demanded the bus driver.

But Paul Townsend was fidgeting. "Look, I don't like
to keep worrying," he said plaintively, "but where *is* this
blonde? She *might* have the poison herself, you know. She
might be in danger. She might be dead. I don't see how
you can talk about Shakespeare and Browning!"

The bus driver said calmly, "She must live within four
or five blocks of this next corner. What time is it?"

"Three twenty. Three twenty-two in fact."

"Yeah, well—not many take olive oil for a snack between
meals."

"Oh, that's *true!*" cried Rosemary, clapping her hands.
"We have more time than we thought."

"Maybe," said Mr. Gibson hopefully but he thought,
within, where a twinge—the pain of life—was creeping.
But there are accidents. He felt a sweet sense of expansion,
and a piercing alarm, all together.

Accidents are possible.

Chapter XVI

THERE WAS a light at the corner of Allen Street and
the Boulevard. Lee Coffey turned right on Allen. Nobody said a word. Paul's car mooched down the first block;
the driver seemed to be testing the very air for the
scent. The car crossed one intersection. Then, in the middle of the second block on Allen, it stopped.

Lee Coffey analyzed the situation aloud. He held his
head down; his eyes were roving; he spoke like a con-
spirator. "*Her* place will be on this side of Allen. Or
around a corner from this side. She waits for the light on
this side of Allen . . . see? If she had to cross, she'd
cross at the Boulevard, see what I mean?"

Mr. Gibson, on the edge of the seat, nodded solemnly. At the same time he felt a little childish pleasure, as if this were a game.

"Now," said Lee, "the first block was all duplexes. Five- and six-room places. But these are private houses, old enough and big enough for taking in roomers." He was right. This second block was an old block. The houses stood up off the ground. Their roofs were up in the tree-tops and the trees were high—conditions not always present in the bursting newness of a California town. "I don't think she's got a lot of dough," he went on, "and I do think she lives by herself. If she had a family, somebody would have a car." This was true in California, U.S.A. "And they'd work it so she wouldn't have to take the bus as much as she does. I get a pretty good idea who rides with me, you know."

"But what can we do," said Paul, "when you don't know her name?"

"What are we going to do, Lee?" asked Rosemary confidently, eagerly. She was on the edge of the seat too.

"This is what we are going to do. We ring doorbells. We take one block at a time. Each of you ask for a blond young lady, not very tall, who is some kind of nurse. Why I say that . . . I've seen her wear white stockings. And, while lots of jobs will take a white uniform, there ain't a female on earth wears white stocking unless she has to. Now, if you find her, or any news of her, give a yell, make a noise to the rest of us. Ask if they've seen her walking by, and if so, which way she turns. But *don't* tell why you're asking." His eye caught Mr. Gibson's wince. "Because it would take too long," the bus driver said. "O.K.?"

This all seemed very logical and clear to everyone. All four of them tumbled out and were deployed. Rosemary ran back along the sidewalk to start at the beginning of the block. Paul went striding far to the left to begin at the end. Lee Coffey started where he was, his nostrils seeming to quiver. He had some reason, Mr. Gibson guessed, to suspect *this* spot, a certain house. A reason he could not or would not explain. Lee Coffey was to work to the left. Mr. Gibson took the next door and would work to the right and meet Rosemary.

He limped up the front walk of the house assigned to him and rang the bell. Nobody answered it; nobody

seemed to be at home. Mr. Gibson stood on the strange
stoop and rang and rang in a dream. (He was Mr. Gibson
of the English Department. No. He was crazy. No, but he
was a criminal. Or he was a man in a desperate plight who
had friends to fight fate for him. How could he let them
down? or let them know that they were doomed? Mr.
Gibson, half dead, half born, was not sure about anything.)

He had just pulled himself together to abandon here
and proceed to ring another when he heard a shrill whistle,
looked, and saw Lee Coffey beckoning with huge gestures
of his long arms.

Mr. Gibson's heart leaped up. He was pleased that Lee
Coffey should be the one of the four of them to find the
scent. He was pleased with the magic of it. It was almost
enough to make you dream a man *could* put intelligence
and intuition against odds and make progress. Which was
romantic and naïve, but he *liked* it. As he limped left-
ward, Rosemary was running to catch up with him and
he saw Paul hurrying back.

They flocked up upon the gray porch of a neat gray
frame house that made one think of New England. There
was even a lilac bush . . . an exotic and difficult plant here
in the West—growing beside the porch railing. In the door
stood a small blond girl at whom Lee Coffey looked down
with hidden eyes.

She was wearing a long wrapper of blue cotton. Her
hair was tousled, as if it had just left a pillow. Her
face was broad at the eyes and curved quickly into a
small chin. It was an attractive little face, not conven-
tionally pretty. The skin was smooth and fine. The mouth
was serious. The gray eyes were serene. The only thing
"blonde" about her, in Ethel's sense, was the color of her
hair.

"And here she is," said Lee, like the Little Bear in the
story.

"What is it, please?" the girl said in a self-assured
voice. She wasn't a person easily surprised, one could
tell. For a slim little girl, she seemed very strong.

Lee blurted, "We aren't here to accuse you, ma'am.
But did you find a bottle of olive oil on a bus today?
And did you bring it home?"

"No, I didn't," said the blonde quietly.

The atmosphere of excited triumphant hope swirled and
began to die down.

"Did you see," said Rosemary doggedly, "my husband . . . this man. . ." she put her hand on Mr. Gibson, "on the bus?"

"No, I didn't" said the blonde. Her eyes traveled from face to face. "Something is wrong? I remember you," she said, coming to Lee Coffey. "Aren't you the driver?" Her eyes were very clear and steady.

"Yes, ma'am." Mr. Gibson found himself waiting for Lee to tell whose blonde she was, but his sandy lashes were discreet.

She wrinkled her fair brow. "Will one of you please tell me what's the matter?"

Rosemary was the one of them who told her. When she was a quarter of the way into the exposition, the small blonde, by gestures only, brought them all inside the house. As if trouble as bad as this better not stand where the breeze might blow and communicate it. So they all sat down in the parlor, on edges of stiff sofas and chairs, while Rosemary went on.

This small blonde female had an air of calm and precision about her. She listened without making noises of alarm or even appreciation. But you knew she did appreciate and was alarmed.

"Then Lee . . . Mr. Coffey, here . . . remembered *you*," finished Rosemary, "and so we came. Hoping you had it. Or had seen something."

"I wouldn't have taken it, I'm sorry, even if I'd seen it. It wouldn't have occurred to me." The blonde's immaculate ringless hands clasped her knee. "I didn't see anything of a paper bag or a bottle." This serene little person had never been in danger from the missing poison.

But now there was no way to continue. They had come to an end. Magic had found the bus driver's blonde, but not the poison. It was not here.

Mr. Gibson squirmed. He found himself incorrigibly on the side of the magic. "You must tell us your name," he said impulsively. He wanted the bus driver to learn her name.

She said her name was Virginia Severson. It suited her. She looked very virginal, and clean, calm, cool in a Scandinavian sort of way. Rosemary rallied and told her all their names. Once again, the civilized ceremony of mutual introduction seemed to relax Paul Townsend. He was charming.

But all this was only delay. The stiff, shabby, spotless parlor seemed airless and stagnant.

Miss Severson said, "I sat pretty well forward in the bus. You must have been sitting behind me." Her grave eyes examined Mr. Gibson. "I'm sorry." She turned her face to Lee Coffey. "You were clever to find me," she said.

"One day," said Lee, "I saw you breathing through a lilac . . ."

"Are you from the East, too?" she said warmly, "that you noticed a lilac?"

"I'll tell you another time," said the bus driver softly, "how come I noticed the lilac."

The blond girl let her lashes down. "I wish I could have helped you," she murmured.

Paul twitched. "Say, if the police have been broadcasting a warning all this time, maybe we should call . . .?"

"Call," said Rosemary with her hands clenched.

Virginia Severson showed Paul the telephone. Mr. Gibson surrendered himself to his chair; hope faded. All the magic belonged to the bus driver. The poison was still lost, still threatening.

The girl came back, biting her lips. "I am a nurse, you know," she said to them. "This . . . well, it shocks me."

"A man has his reasons," said Lee Coffey, gently. "It's easy to say he was crazy. It's also lazy."

Virginia Severson tilted her head and shot him a glance that was suddenly alert. "His reasons aren't the question, right now, are they?" she said. "I meant unlabeled poison, Mr. Coffey. Floating around. That's *shocking!* I'm trained to be careful with drugs."

"We'd like to find it, Miss Severson. We'd mighty like to find it," he drawled. His intent gaze was challenging.

"Of course, you would," she said. "*I* would, too." She seemed to feel the force of his challenge. "Let me try to think . . ." she said soberly and sat down, pulling the long blue around her pretty feet.

Paul came back and spoke reluctantly to Rosemary's yearning face. "Nothing." He looked nervous and defeated. "Not a word. It's three thirty. Where *is* that stuff?"

"It's somewhere," said Rosemary with a little gasp. *"Somewhere!"*

Mr. Gibson found himself pushing his imagination, too,

trying to picture the bottle in the green bag . . . *some-where*. But where?

"Rosie, this is too tough," said Paul. "I don't think we're accomplishing anything."

"Yes, we are. Be quiet," said Lee Coffey reverently, "Virginia is thinking." The nurse smiled at him. She had a lovely smile, and the bus driver let his face look fond.

"Lee . . ." said Rosemary, her voice ready to break, "Miss . . . Virginia. It's no time for . . ."

"We're not," said the bus driver quickly.

Mr. Gibson understood perfectly. But Paul Townsend didn't. His tall frame remained in the archway and his handsome face wore a lost expression as if to say, But what are you all talking about? Virginia had understood too, Mr. Gibson guessed, as her lids went down again. And Virginia *agreed*.

How remarkably quickly, thought Mr. Gibson, things *can* be communicated. Lee Coffey has told this girl he's long noticed her, has liked her looks, likes her now, and expects a good deal of her. And she has told him she is . . . not offended. She would even like to deserve his good opinion. She already knows this is an interesting man. Yet both of them resolve that they will not pursue this enchantment . . . that, first, they will help me if they can. A bus driver, he thought. A blonde. His eyes stung suddenly.

Nobody spoke. Until the little nurse said, at last, in her quiet unexcited voice, "There was somebody *I* know, on the bus. Would that help?"

"Oh yes, it might," cried Rosemary, jumping up. "Oh yes! Oh, good for you!"

"You see?" said Lee Coffey.

"Mrs. Boatright was on that bus," the nurse told them, getting to her feet. "Mrs. Boatright. I remember now, wondering how three or four cars could all be unavailable, at once. She had a heap of packages, too. On the bus. It seemed strange. She's so very wealthy . . . at least her husband is. She lives in a huge place on the hill. I'm sure it was she. I once met her at Red Cross headquarters."

"Walter Boatright . . ." Lee Coffey sprang up and dove into the hallway and came back with the phone book.

"But I'm afraid *she'd* have an unlisted number," Virginia said. "In fact, I know she has."

"*Not* what the number *is?*" The bus driver lowered the book.

"No. Sorry."

"Do you know the house?"

"Yes, but not the street number, either."

"Can't we go there?" Rosemary cried. And Paul half groaned and the bus driver looked at his blonde.

"You all start," Virginia said. She was already at a plain white door the far side of the room. "Don't wait. I'll catch you at the car."

Lee Coffey grinned and glanced at his watch, and then took Mr. Gibson by one wing. "Is she a blonde?" he murmured, almost carrying Mr. Gibson down the porch steps past the lilac bush. "Do you blame me?"

"She's a lovely blonde," said Mr. Gibson, overwhelmed. "This is so good of you."

"And all for money, too," said Rosemary tartly. "All for material advantage." Mr. Gibson looked at his wife, who had his other arm. Her blue eyes were bright.

"Listen, we got our teeth in it now," said Lee with enormous gusto.

"We're going to find it," said Rosemary.

Mr. Gibson could almost believe this.

Chapter XVII

THEY STUFFED HIM into the tonneau and Rosemary sprang in, too. She shoved over, and Lee Coffey, using nothing but an air of expectancy, stuffed Paul Townsend in at the other side of Rosemary. Then he slipped into the driver's seat and turned the key. The motor caught. The door of the house opened. Virginia skipped down the walk, wearing a brown jumper over a white blouse, brown pumps on her bare feet; her blond hair was neat and shining. The bus driver grinned and let the car move just as she slipped in beside him. He had not waited even one-tenth of a second. She had not failed him either.

Paul said admiringly, "That was a quick change!"

Nobody paid any attention to him. It would have been better not to have commented.

As the car moved, the little nurse began to describe the location of the house they were seeking, and Lee sent them spinning around the block, across the Boulevard, and on north. They were heading for a swelling slope in the northwest section of the town where lawns grew wider and houses larger as they stood higher on the hill. Mrs. Boatright's house, she said, would be close to the top, on a short street, where there were only three or four houses, and hers had vast lawns behind a wall.

"The higher the fewer, I guess," said Paul.

Virginia turned to look back. "Is there an antidote to this poison, Mr. Townsend?" she said in a professional kind of way.

"Paul," he suggested.

She smiled at him. "What ought to be done . . . in case . . . ?"

"I'm afraid *I* don't know of any antidote," Paul confessed, sliding forward in the seat, the other side of Rosemary. "Of course I'm no doctor. All we understand, in our business, is what the danger is. We're trained to be careful, too."

"How did he ever get hold of it?" the nurse frowned.

Paul told her. As Mr. Gibson listened, he began to know that Paul Townsend was projecting himself somehow and being quite skillfully charming to this most attractive little person. Mr. Gibson found himself curiously affronted.

He looked at Rosemary, dear Rosemary, who sat still between them with her hands clenched . . . whose resolution was their strength, who had begun this fight and fired them all from her own spirit and collected these valiant lieutenants.

He said, "What a fighter you are, Rosemary!"

"I am a rabbit," she said bitterly. "I was always a rabbit. I should have begun to fight long, long ago."

Paul turned and covered her tense hands with one of his. "Now, now, Rosie . . . try to take it easy. You'll make yourself sick. Worry doesn't help any, does it, Virginia?"

The nurse did not answer. The bus driver said, "She's getting a lot of mileage out of her worry. Hey, Rosemary?"

"Yes, thank you," said Rosemary, rather forlornly, collapsing a little from her rigidity. Paul took his hand away. "I'm worrying now," she said, "trying to imagine a wealthy woman picking up a strange package on a public bus. I don't suppose she would."

"She might," said the nurse brightly. "By mistake, you see? Suppose she gathered it up with the other packages she was carrying. I didn't see her get off. I got off first. But who can say? And suppose she had things to eat in her own packages? She might dump them all in the kitchen. And she surely has servants. Her cook, for instance, wouldn't *know*. Her cook might think Mrs. Boatright had meant to bring home some olive oil."

"A *little* bottle?" said Rosemary pathetically. "A very *small* quantity? What time is it?"

"Three thirty-seven," Paul told her.

"It's still early, anyhow," said Rosemary, with a desperate smile.

But Mr. Gibson thought, It's late. He thought of time gone by. Time enough for someone to have died already and very mysteriously, too. So that the news of the result might not yet have caught up with the cause. This fight might already have been lost, for all they knew.

"The Boatright kids are in their teens," said the nurse thoughtfully. "They certainly wouldn't be fed their supper this early."

"Olive oil?" said Rosemary. "What would a cook *do* with it?"

The nurse said, "Salad? Oh . . . to moisten a sandwich filling . . . possibly for a snack . . ."

"Don't say that!" said Paul.

The nurse said, "I guess I'm helping her worry."

". . . Resembles thought," muttered the bus driver.

But Mr. Gibson was appalled. A child! Oh, if a child were to get the poison! He said aloud, "All of you ought to leave me. You are very good to trouble yourselves—"

"No trouble," said Virginia. Mr. Gibson discovered that he believed her. "I believe you," he said to her in surprise and she smiled.

"Don't worry," Paul began.

"Stop saying that," said Rosemary quietly. "It doesn't help, Paul."

"I told you, Rosie," he said rather crossly, "you ought to have talked to him, laid things on the line . . ."

"You did. You told me. You were right," said Rosemary, looking straight ahead. "Yes, Paul." Her hands twitched.

"You musta seen something brewing, Rosemary," the bus driver said sympathetically, not quite understanding. He hadn't the background. "A man doesn't decide in a day."

(But I did, mused Mr. Gibson, wonderingly. In a night. I seemed to.)

"Have you been ill, Mr. Gibson?" the nurse asked, "or taking drugs for pain? I see you limping."

Mr. Gibson was bewildered. (His heart hurt. He wasn't dead at all.) "A broken bone or two," he murmured. "Just an accident." Rosemary turned her face to look at his. He looked away.

"I only wondered," said Virginia gently. "There *are* illnesses that can be very depressing. And some drugs, too."

Mr. Gibson, gazing at a curb whizzing by, thought *Doom,* yes. Here comes doom, again.

"I was depressed," he said without spirit. "That's a name for it."

"If you had only seen a doctor," the nurse scolded him delicately, with her soft regret. "So often a doctor can help these depressed feelings."

"By a little tinkering in the machinery?" said Mr. Gibson rather bitterly.

"They do know how to help sometimes," the nurse said, rather mechanically. She seemed to be tasting, perhaps diagnosing this answer.

"You go for this psychosomatic stuff?" inquired the bus driver abruptly.

"Don't you?" she said.

"Long ago," he declaimed, "long ago *I* threw a whole bunch of arbitrary distinctions outa my head. Either—or. Body or mind. Matter or spirit. Hah! *Now* it turns out matter is *less* solid than spirit, far as I can figure what they're talking. Nothing's any more un-gross than the human body. Or a chair, either. Zillions of cells—atoms and subdivisions of same—whizzing around, and . . . *they* made outa what? Waves. Rhythms. Time itself, for all we know. Caution to the jaybirds," he concluded.

Virginia laughed out loud, delightedly.

But Mr. Gibson was on his way down for the second time. *Doom,* he said to himself, and aloud, "I suppose I was ill. At least that's a name for what I was."

"Now," said Virginia. "Look, we are so ignorant."

"Yes, we are ignorant," said Rosemary gladly.

"Anybody who knows anything at all about medical science—or any other, I guess—only *begins* to know how ignorant we are," said Virginia. She looked brightly back at Mr. Gibson. She expected him to be glad.

"Where there's life there's hope, you mean?" said Paul. He seemed to think he was joining in.

The nurse frowned. Her small chin was almost resting upon the back of the front seat as she sat twisted around to talk to them. "I meant we know enough to know there's an *awful* lot more to be found out. We do know just a little bit about how to find it. Don't you *see*, Mr. Gibson? There are people looking for ways to help all the time and they've found some. I've seen. Nobody knows what they *might* find out by tomorrow morning. You should have asked for help," she chided.

"So should I," said Rosemary not very loudly.

Mr. Gibson didn't reply. He was busy perceiving something odd. It was hard to fit into the structure of doom. That was what was odd about it. Say the individual is depressed because of his internal chemistry, call it his machinery. *Even so*. He is not *quite* doomed . . . not if his fellow men, men who hold their minds open because they humbly know their ignorance . . . not if these have discovered even *some* helpful things to do for him. And this was strange, a strange weakness—wasn't it?—in the huge hard jaws of doom.

"That's funny," he said aloud.

Nobody asked him what he meant and he did not tell. The car slid up a tree-lined street and all the passengers were silent for a block.

Then Paul fidgeted. "I should have called home. I wonder if Jeanie got back . . . and Mama's O.K."

"It must be nearly four o'clock," said Rosemary. "Ethel will be home." She lifted her head, it was almost as if she tossed it haughtily.

Ethel! Gibson felt shocked. What would Ethel say? He couldn't even imagine. Absolutely nothing that had happened since eleven o'clock this morning had made Ethel's kind of sense.

"*I* don't think he was ill," the bus driver blurted. "*I* think he was shook."

Virginia tilted her head to look at him respectfully.

"To his foundations," said the bus driver.

"But everybody loved him," said Rosemary, and raised her clenched hands like a desperate prayer.

"Why sure, everybody thought a hell of a lot of Gibson," said Paul indignantly, as if Mr. Gibson had offended unpardonably.

"Everybody?" said the bus driver ruminatively. "Now, let's not promise candy."

"Candy?" said the nurse with curiosity.

"He had *something* on his mind; it wasn't hardly just missing the brotherly love of his fellow man," said Lee. "Hey? And look, honeybunch," he said to his blonde, "we are now on Hathaway Drive, so where's this mansion?"

"It's the white Colonial," said Virginia.

Rosemary said, "Maybe the poison is here."

Mr. Gibson was a chip in a current. He got out of the car with all the rest of them.

They had pulled up within the wall, in the wide spot where the drive curved before the pillared entrance. The wide and spanking-white façade looked down upon them, and all the exquisite ruffles of the dainty window curtains announced that here money, and many hired hands, made order.

Now Virginia took the lead. She rang the bell. A maid-servant opened the door. "Is Mrs. Boatright here? We must see her quickly. It's very important." Virginia's crisp grave manner was impressive.

The maid said, "Come in, please," looking as unsurprised as she was able. She left them standing on the oriental rug of the wide foyer. To their left was a huge room. A pair of saddle oxfords hung over the arm of a gray-and-yellow couch, which shoes wiggled, being attached to a pair of young feet. There must be a girl, flat on her back on the sofa. She was talking. There was no one else in there. She must be talking on the telephone.

A boy, about sixteen years old, came in a jumping gallop down the broad stairs. "Oh, hi!" said he, and romped off to their right, where there was another room, and a lot of books and a piano. The boy snatched up a horn and they heard some melancholy toots receding.

Then Mrs. Walter Boatright, in person, sailed out of a white door under the stairs. She was about five and a half feet tall and about two and a half feet wide. Every ounce under the beige-cotton-and-white-lace was firm. She had short white hair, nicely waved, and a thin nose made a prow for the well-fleshed face. Her eyes were blue (although not so blue as Rosemary's) and they were simply interested. "Yes? Oh, Miss Severson. How do you do?"

Virginia gave a little start at being called her own name, but she omitted any more preliminaries. "I saw you on a bus, today, ma'am . . ."

"I'm so sorry," cut in Mrs. Boatright, her words mechanical, while her eyes still inquired and expected. "Had I seen *you*, my dear . . ."

The little nurse brushed this aside. "Please. Did you pick up a small green paper bag by mistake?"

"I doubt it," said Mrs. Boatright, accepting the abrupt manner as urgency without showing a ripple in her poise. "Now shall we just see?" She turned. Her bulk moved with surprising ease and grace. "Mona."

Mona turned out to be the maid.

"Ask Geraldine if I brought in a small green paper bag."

"Yes, Mrs. Boatright."

"What is in the bag?" inquired the lady of the house of her callers.

Virginia told her.

Mrs. Boatright compressed her lips. "Yes, I see. This is serious," said she. "Dell." The girl on the phone bobbed up, using the muscles at her waist, and said, "Hold on a sec, Christy. Yoo, Ma?"

"Put up the phone," said Mrs. Boatright. "We'll need it. Get Tom. Tell him to search his car carefully for a small green paper bag with a bottle in it."

"Yes, Ma. . . . Call you back, Christy. Bye now."

"My son picked me up at the bus stop," said Mrs. Boatright in explanation, meanwhile sailing toward the phone.

The girl, Dell, who was perhaps eighteen, went across before them in a gait like dancing. Her eyes were curious but smiling.

A woman in a blue uniform came out of the white door. "No ma'am," said she. "No green paper bag in the kitchen at all."

"Thank you, Geraldine," said Mrs. Boatright and then into the phone, "The police, if you please?" She said to the five of them, who all stood speechless watching her operate, "Which of you is Mr. Gibson?"

Mr. Gibson felt himself being pointed out from all sides. He stood in a dream, not miserable enough, but rather guiltily fascinated.

"Police?" said Mrs. Boatright. "Has the poison in the olive oil been located yet? . . . Thank you." Mrs. Boatright put the phone up and wasted no more time than she had words. "Not yet," she said. "Yes, you *were* on the bus with me. Now, what can I do?"

"It's been a chain," said Rosemary, quivering between disappointment and hope. "The driver remembered *her*. *She* remembered *you*."

"And I," said Mrs. Boatright (who had not yet said "Oh dear" or "How terrible") "remember Theo Marsh." She nodded and held them in order with a kind of invisible gavel. "But, first, let's be *sure*."

"Not a thing in my car, Ma," said the boy, Tom, reappearing. He looked at the group with curiosity but did not ask questions.

"Who . . . ?"

"Marsh?"

"Where . . . ?"

Mrs. Boatright rapped the air for order. "The only way to reach Theo Marsh that I know of," said she, "is to drive out there. He has no phone in his studio. The man isolates himself to work." She saw their ignorance. "He is the painter, of course."

"Where is this studio?" asked Lee and added, "madame?"

"Can I describe it to the police, I wonder?" Mrs. Boatright gathered her brows.

"Can't we *go*?" said Rosemary. "We've already been so far. It's better than waiting . . ."

"Might be quicker," Lee said, "Surer."

Mrs. Boatright said, "As a matter of fact, it might be wiser. Theo Marsh might, just whimsically, lie low and refuse to admit a policeman. But he knows me." One felt nobody could lie low, if Mrs. Boatright chose otherwise. "Now," the lady turned lightly on her heel, "both Cadillacs are at the garage and won't be available 'til six o'clock. Walter was forced to take Dell's car. It seems, Tom, we must use yours."

The boy looked as dashed as if his mother had proposed removing his trousers to lend them to a tramp.

"We have a car, madame," the bus driver said, his

sandy lashes somehow admiring her, "and there's still half a tank of gas in her."

"And an excellent driver," Virginia said.

"Very well," said Mrs. Boatright. "Mona, bring me my tan jacket, please, and my bag." She made another of her swift turns. "Meantime, Tom, search the house for a bottle of olive oil in a green paper bag. By no means touch the contents. It is poison. Geraldine, serve dinner at six-thirty; I may be late. Dell . . ." (The girl was back.) "Call your father. Say I am called away. At seven, if I am not here, call Mr. Coster of the Board of Education and say I am unavoidably detained. Call Mrs. Peters and tell her I may not have the lists for her until tomorrow. Apologize." She took her jacket from the hands of the maid who had hopped to do as she was bidden. "Let's go," said Mrs. Walter Boatright. She sailed out of her front door and the five of them straggled along in her wake.

The bus driver got under the wheel and tucked his blonde beside him and Paul got into the right front seat.

Mrs. Boatright let Rosemary go first into the tonneau while she turned and said to her son, "Keep Dell off the phone. I may call."

"Gosh, Ma, give me something easy," the boy said.

His mother flipped her hand farewell and she got in and Mr. Gibson, last, beside her.

"Where to?" said the bus driver respectfully.

"Go out the Boulevard," said Mrs. Boatright, "all the way to the end of the bus line. Theo Marsh has a studio in the country. Quite a hideaway. But I believe I know the turn. If not, we can inquire at the junction."

The car was moving already.

"I don't just remember anybody who looked like a *painter*," Lee said, "getting off the end of the line. You mean, a fine-art-type painter?"

"If he got off sooner," said Mrs. Boatright, "we cannot know where he was heading, and there is no use wondering about it. We must go on what we know."

"Sure thing," said Lee. "That's abso-tootly right."

"Very rustic, that studio," Mrs. Boatright continued. "The man's a fine painter, yes. But I'm just afraid . . ."

"Afraid?" Rosemary's voice sounded tired. Mr. Gibson couldn't see her now. Not with Mrs. Boatright in the middle.

"If Theo Marsh, of all people, found a bottle of olive oil on a bus . . . I assume it *was* imported?"

"Yes," said Mr. Gibson.

"*He* would accept it joyously, as a gift from the gods, and he, and that model of his, would add it to some feast or other with no hesitation. What a loss it would be!" said Mrs. Boatright. "A fine artist! We can't spare *them*."

"What time is it?" asked Rosemary tensely.

"Only four o'clock . . . just about one minute after," Paul told them. "Too early for supper."

"Alas," said Mrs. Boatright, "I imagine Theo Marsh will eat when he is hungry .I doubt if the man has names for meals."

"Is it very far?" asked Rosemary pathetically.

"Thirty minutes," promised Lee Coffey. "Do *I* know that boulevard!"

The car picked up its heels and scooted rapidly down curving streets.

"Now what's all this," said Mrs. Boatright severely, "about suicide?"

Mr. Gibson put his hand over his eyes.

"Ever since Ethel came," said Rosemary passionately. "Ever since *she* came! I don't know what she's done to him. I was too upset by what she did to me."

"You are his wife, my dear?"

"Yes, I am," said Rosemary as defiantly as if somebody else had claimed the title.

"And our driver is the driver of the bus, is he not?" Mrs. Boatright was proceeding with order, ignoring outbursts. "And the other gentleman?"

"I am their neighbor," said Paul. "Townsend is my name."

"And our friend," said Rosemary with a forced sweetness as if she were struggling to keep polite and calm.

"And Miss Severson was a passenger?" Mrs. Boatright sailed right on, "Does anyone remember the tale of the Golden Goose?"

"Hey!" said the bus driver. "Sure, I remember. Everybody who takes ahold has to tag along. That's pretty good, Mrs. Boatright."

"But who is Ethel?" Mrs. Boatright had come around a curve and would have all clear.

"Ethel," said Rosemary in a desperately even tone, "is Kenneth's sister, a good woman, a fine person, who came here to help and to take care of us, after we had an accident . . ." Her voice rose. "I shouldn't have said what I did. But I can't—I cannot be grateful any more. It's no time to be grateful. It just doesn't count any more." The strain was telling and Rosemary began to cry. "This terrible trouble and it's getting late and I'd so *hate* it to be an artist . . . way out in the country and no help nearby . . ."

Mr. Gibson, too, could see, ahead of them, a rustic studio strewn with bodies.

"There wouldn't be much help," said Paul miserably. "That stuff works fast."

"Now, we'll see, when we get there," said Mrs. Boatright, "and not before. Mr. Coffey is making the best possible time. We are doing the best possible thing."

"It's so long . . ." wept Rosemary.

So Mrs. Boatright, who was in equal parts mother *and* commanding officer, took Rosemary to her bosom and began to stroke her hair. Mr. Gibson felt a tremendous relief. He blessed Mrs. Boatright. The three heads in the front seat were still, facing forward.

"Gratitude," said the bus driver suddenly, "is for the birds. There's all kinds of ins and outs to this, Mrs. Boatright, and we don't know the half of them. But this Ethel —see, Mrs. Boatright?—she puts it into Rosemary's head that Rosemary meant to get him smashed up in an auto accident, which is why he is limping, did you notice? Well, this Ethel, she's got poor Rosemary feeling guilty as hell because she was driving at the time, although it was a pure and simple accident . . . but this Ethel she's the kind who knows better than you do what your real motives were, see? And Rosemary thinks she shouldn't get mad at Ethel, because this Ethel shows up to help and all and besides this Ethel is her sister-in-law and I don't guess Rosemary *likes* squabbling with the relatives. Some people thrive on that. Hey? Some people make a career out of it."

"I see. I see," said Mrs. Boatright, stopping his flow. "Had you seen much of this sister-in-law before?"

"Never," wailed Rosemary.

"Let her cry," said Virginia. "Cry hard, Rosemary."

Paul squirmed. "Look . . . she can't take much more of this . . ."

"It's high time she bawled her head off," the nurse said fiercely. "And Mr. Gibson, too."

But Mr. Gibson sat, dry-eyed and amazed.

"I'm sorry . . ." sobbed Rosemary. "It isn't really Ethel, herself. I know that. But it's her ideas. It's the way she thinks. And what can you do? I know I'm a rabbit but, even if you aren't a rabbit, how can you fight that kind of thing? I've told myself . . . I've told her . . . I couldn't have meant it. But the idea is, *I* wouldn't know if I had! I'd be the *last* to know! And how can you argue with somebody who just turns everything you say *around?* Who just makes you feel as if every time you opened your mouth you were giving some horrible inner beastly self away? If you insist, *she* thinks Aha, you protest too much! So you *must* really mean the exact *opposite*. If you talk loud, because you feel so strongly that you're right . . . why, a loud voice means you must be trying to sell yourself a lie. It's maddening," said Rosemary. "You can't *know* anything. You can't trust yourself, at all."

Doomed, said Mr. Gibson in his throat or his mind. Nobody seemed to hear him.

"What I'd like to know," said Lee Coffey angrily, "is who gives this Ethel her license to read minds. Hey? *I'd* give Rosemary a fifty-fifty chance to know, as well as Ethel, what Rosemary means by what she says."

"No, you *can't*," wept Rosemary. "You're the *last*. That's the paralyzing thing!"

The nurse said some angry syllable under her breath. The driver's head agreed savagely.

"Gratitude," said Mrs. Boatright, rhythmically stroking Rosemary's hair with one plump jeweled hand, "lasts on, for a time, after the deed that caused it. But it's like a fire, don't you think so? It's lit, it burns, it's warm. But it needs fuel. It doesn't last forever unless it's fed."

Mrs. Boatright was making a speech. She had a clear voice and she knew how to breathe and she could be rather eloquent. Even Rosemary stopped her weeping noises to listen.

"No one should be the prisoner of stale gratitude—to change and also *mix* the metaphor" declaimed Mrs. Boatright. "I think of the children in this world, enslaved by parents trading on gratitude for old deeds that should have been done for love only in the first place. I think of parents who have become, in fact, whining nuisances that flesh-and-blood rightfully resents and yet blood, that is thicker than water, scourges itself for resenting. I shudder at so much unhappiness. Gratitude can be a dreadful thing when it becomes a debt—you see?—and there is guilt and reluctance. But if, by continued feeding, faith is created, and mutual respect is accumulated and confidence grows, in love, in friendship, then gratitude turns into something better. And something durable." She paused and one expected the pattering of ladies' hands over the luncheon tables. Here was only the rushing sound of the car, and Rosemary saying, "I know . . ." in a choking voice.

"If parents, for instance," said Mrs. Boatright, wistfully, in a more private kind of voice, "could only grow up to be their children's friends . . . Have you children, my dear?"

Paul said hastily, almost in alarm. "They've only been married . . . less than three months . . ."

There was a silence, deep . . . except for the sounds of the car's progress.

Lee Coffey said in a moment, "Is that so? I didn't know that."

"A bride and a groom," said Virginia slowly, her voice caressing the words sadly.

The news was sinking into the fabric of all their speculations, dyeing everything to different colors. Mr. Gibson felt like crying out, No, you don't understand. It was only a silly, unrealistic arrangement. And I am fifty-five. She is thirty-two. It leaves twenty-three.

He cried out nothing.

Mrs. Boatright turned and said to him, "Rosemary finds your sister difficult. Rosemary has been unhappy. But Rosemary wasn't the one who stole the poison, was she?"

"No," he said. "No."

"Then what was the matter with *you?*" she asked.

He couldn't answer.

Paul turned around. "You certainly raised the devil," he said. "You might have been a little bit thoughtful of Rosie at least. *And* Ethel. And *me,* for that matter. If you'd thought of others and not yourself . . ."

"He does think of others," said Rosemary faintly.

"Not today, he didn't," said Paul, "and what he did was a sin." He jerked his head to look forward. The back of his neck was righteous and furious.

" 'Oh . . . that the Everlasting had not fixed His canon 'gainst self-slaughter . . .' " crooned the bus driver. "That's what you mean, hey?"

"You know what I mean."

"Yes, but that's *our* culture," said the bus driver. "You take Japan . . ."

"*You* take Japan," said Paul, sulkily.

Mrs. Boatright, who had a way of going back and clearing up one thing at a time, said, "I serve with the Red Cross, the Board of Education, the Society for the Encouragement of the U.N., the Council for Juvenile Welfare, the American Women for Political Housecleaning, and the church, of course, and I work in these groups. But not for 'others.' Isn't this *my* world? And while I am here, *my* business?" She conquered her oratorical impulses. "There is a weakness about that word 'others,' " she said privately, "and I never have liked it."

"It's not definitive," snapped Virginia. "Show me one patient. *An* other."

"The odds ain't good," said Lee Coffey ruminatively. "Couple of billion 'others'; only one of you. You *can't* take an interest, except pretty vague and slightly phony, in the whole caboodle of 'em."

"Quite so," said Mrs. Boatright genially. "You can only start from where you are."

"Although once you get into this business," said Virginia softly, "you are led on."

"One thing comes after another," agreed the bus driver, and the nurse looked at him, with that quick alert tilt of her head again.

"Do you get paid, Mrs. Boatright?" said Rosemary, straightening up suddenly.

"Of course not." Mrs. Boatright was scandalized.

"You see? She's just a parasite," said Rosemary, half hysterically.

"Hey!" crowed Lee Coffey. "That sounds like good old Ethel to me. Ethel says any dame whose old man has got dough is just a parasite? I'll betcha she does. So she never met a high-powered executive like Mrs. B. I'm telling you, this Ethel has got everything bass-ackward. Hey, what was it she said about blondes? You never did tell me."

"Blondes," said Rosemary clearly, "are predatory nitwits."

"Are-ent they, though?" said Lee to his nurse fondly. "Aren't they just? *All* of 'em. This means you, too, honeybunch. You and your definitive, your patient." He chuckled. "Oh boy, you know, that's Ethel's trouble, right there? She starts out with 'some,' slides into 'many,' and don't notice herself skidding right off the rails into 'all.' "

"Ethel's a pain in the neck," said Paul grumpily. "I told you, Rosie, the day she sent you into a fit—"

"Ethel," put in Mrs. Boatright thoughtfully, "is beginning to sound like a scapegoat."

Mr. Gibson stirred himself and said rather sharply, "Yes. And you are all so very kind to be pro-me; I can't think why. . . . But I'd like to get this straight, please. *I* stole the poison. *I* meant to die. *I* stupidly, criminally, left it on the bus. *I* am responsible, guilty, wrong, and totally to blame." He *knew* this to be true.

"Yes," said the bus driver in a moment, thoughtfuly, "when you come right down to it, *sure* you are."

But Mr. Gibson was thinking dizzily . . . Yes, but if I am to blame, there was freedom. I could have done otherwise. Without freedom, there is no blame. And vice versa. His brain swam. I don't know, he thought. I thought I knew but I don't know.

"Not a lot of use in blame, though," the bus driver was saying. "It shouldn't linger. You shouldn't blow on *them* ashes, hey, Mrs. B.?"

"Make a note of an error," said that matron briskly, "for future reference . . . but file it. Now, Rosemary, powder your nose and put on some lipstick and brace up. Theo Marsh may very well be lost in some masterpiece with the thought of nourishment far, far from his mind. It would be quite like him."

"I haven't got a lipstick," wailed Rosemary.

"Use mine," said Virginia warmly.

"Put a good face on it, girls," said the bus driver tolerantly. "A man, he takes a shave . . ."

Mr. Gibson saw Paul Townsend rubbing his jaw.

The whole thing struck him. The six of them, this heterogeneous crew, hurtling out into the country on a guess and a prayer, and conversing so fantastically.

Mr. Gibson heard a rusty chuckle coming out of him. "You know," he said, "this is remarkable?"

Not a one of them agreed. He felt all their eyes, Lee's in the rear-vision miror, Virginia's and Paul's turning back, Mrs. Boatright's at his side, Rosemary peering around her. All the eyes said, What do you mean? Not at all!

"Are we getting there?" said Rosemary.

"We are," said Mrs. Boatright.

When they passed the place where the yellow bus had been left, on the road's shoulder, it was gone. Lee said, "Hey, I wonder am I fired?" No one could tell him, and since he had sounded merely, and rather merrily, curious to know, no one tried to console him, either.

After a while Mrs. Boatright said, "It's a dirt road. Going off to the right a few yards beyond the junction. The house is wood, stained brown, and it sits on a knoll."

"I can *see* a house like that," said Virginia. "Look. Is that it? Up there?"

Chapter XVIII

THE LOW STRUCTURE on the high knoll looked not only rustic but abandoned. The front wall was blank. Weeds grew up to the doorstep. On a narrow terrace of old brick, overrun by wild grass, a few dilapidated redwood outdoor chairs sat at careless angles, their cushions faded and torn. A cat leaped out of one of these and fled into the wilderness.

No sound, no sign of life came from this building.

Mrs. Boatright rapped smartly.

Without sound, the door swung inward. They could see directly into a huge room and the north and opposite wall was glass, so that this space was flooded with clear and steady light. The first thing Mr. Gibson saw was a body.

The body was that of a female in a long flaring skirt of royal blue *and nothing else*. It was lying on a headless couch. As he blinked his dazzled eyes, it sat up. The naked torso writhed. It was alive.

A man's living voice said, "What have we here? Mary Anne Boatright! Well! Is this a club?"

The torso was pulling on a loose white T-shirt, slightly ragged at the shoulder seams. It went strangely with the rich silk of the skirt and the skirt's gold-embroidered hem.

"This is important," said Mrs. Boatright, "or I wouldn't disturb you, Theo."

"I should hope it is," said the voice. "It better be. Never mind. I'm tired. I just decided. Put your shirt on, Lavinia."

"I did, already," said the girl or woman on the couch who was sitting there like a lump, now. She turned her bare feet until they rested pigeon-toed, one over the other. Her eyes were huge and dark and placid as a cow's.

Mr. Gibson tore his gaze away from her to see this man.

"Theodore Marsh," said Mrs. Boatright formally, but rapidly. "This is Mrs. Gibson, Miss Severson, Mr. Gibson, Mr. Townsend, Mr. Coffey."

"You don't look like a club," said the painter. "What are you? I've surely seen several of you before, somewhere."

He was tall and skinny as a scarecrow. He wore tweed trousers, a pink shirt, and a black vest. His hair was pure white and it looked as if it had never been brushed but remained in a state of nature, like fur. His face was wizened and shrewd, his hands knobby. He must have been seventy.

He was full of energy. He moved, flipperty-flop, all angles, beckoning them in. He had yellow teeth, all but three, which were too white to match the rest, and obviously false. His grin made one think of an ear of corn peculiarly both white and golden. He certainly had not been poisoned.

"Did you find a bottle of olive oil?" Rosemary attacked in a rush.

"Not I. Sit," he said. "Explain."

Mr. Gibson sat down, feeling weak and breathless. The nurse and the bus driver sat down, side by side. Paul remained standing, for his manners. His eyes avoided the sight of the model's bare feet.

Mrs. Boatright, standing, her corsets firm, told the painter the story succinctly and efficiently. Rosemary, by her side, punctuated all she said with wordless gestures of anxiety.

Theo Marsh subdued his energy long enough to listen quickly, somehow. He got the situation into his mind, whole and fast.

"Yes, I was on a bus. Took it in front of the public library late this morning. You the driver? I did not study your face."

"Few do." Lee shrugged.

"Can you help us?" interrupted Rosemary impatiently. "Did you see a green paper bag, Mr. Marsh? Or did you see who took it?"

The artist took his gaze off the bus driver and put it upon Rosemary. He leaned his head sharply to the right as if to see how she would look upside down. "I may have seen it," he said calmly. "I see a lot. I'll tell you, in a minute. Let me get the pictures back."

Mrs. Boatright took a throne. At least she deposited her weight upon a chair so regally that it might as well have been one.

"You, with the worries and the graceful backbone," the painter said, "sit down. And don't wiggle. I despise wiggling women. I must not be distracted, mind."

Rosemary sat down in the only remaining place, on the couch beside the model. She sat . . . and her spine *was* graceful . . . as still as a mouse.

(Mouse, thought Mr. Gibson. Oh, how have we come here, you and I, who surely meant no harm?)

Six of them, plus the model Lavinia, all stared solemnly at Theo Marsh. He enjoyed this. *He* didn't seat himself. He moved, flippety-flop, all elbows and angles, up and down.

"G-green," stammered Mr. Gibson.

"Green?" the painter sneered. "Look out the window."

Mr. Gibson looked, blinked, said, "Yes?"

"There are at least thirty-five different and distinct greens framed there. I know. I counted. I put them on canvas. So tell me, what color was the bag?"

"It was a kind of . . ." said Mr. Gibson feebly. "—well, greenish . . ."

"They have eyes and see not," mourned the painter. "All right." He began to act like a machine gun, shooting words.

"Pine green?"

"No."

"Yellow green? Chartreuse? You've heard of that?"

"No. It wasn't—"

"Grass green?"

"No."

"Kelly green?"

"Theo," said Mrs. Boatright warningly.

"Am I showing off, Mary Anne?" The painter grinned.

"Yes," said Mrs. Boatright.

"Well then, truce to that." The painter shrugged. "Well then, gray green?"

"Y-yes," said Mr. Gibson, struggling. "Palish, dullish . . ."

"In other words, paper-bag green," said the painter, amiably. "Of course." He rambled to the left and stopped still and looked blind. "I sat on the left side of the bus," he said dreamily. "For the first ten minutes I examined a hat. What blossoms! Watermelon shade. Nine petals, which is *un*likely. Well, to proceed. I saw you . . . the man there with the good eyes. That can't tell one green from another."

"Me?" squeaked Mr. Gibson.

"A man of sorrows, thought I," the painter continued. "Oh yes, you did have in your left hand a gray-green paper bag."

Mr. Gibson began to tremble.

"I watched you a while. How I envied you your youth and your sorrow! I said to myself, this man is really living!"

Mr. Gibson thought one of them must have gone mad!

The artist's eyes slid under half-drawn lids. "I saw you put the paper bag down on the seat." The eyes were nearly closed now, and yet watched. "You took a small black covered notebook out of your pocket . . ."

"I . . . did?"

"You produced a gold ball-point pen, about five inches long, and you wrote—brooded—wrote . . ."

"I did!" Mr. Gibson began to feel all his pockets.

"Then you got to brooding so bad you forgot to write. I lost interest. Nothing more to see, you know. Besides, I discovered an ear without a lobe, two seats ahead of me."

Rosemary had jumped up. She stood over Mr. Gibson as he drew his little pocket notebook out and flipped the pages. Yes, pen marks. He looked at what he had written on the bus. "Rosemary . . . Rosemary . . . Rosemary." Nothing but her name three times. That was all.

"Trying . . . a letter to you," he stammered, and looked up.

Rosemary's eyes were enigmatic . . . perhaps sad. She shook her head slightly, walked slowly back to the couch and sat down. Lavinia changed her feet, and put the top one underneath.

"I saw *you*, Mary Anne," the painter said, "and pretended not. I lay low. Forgive me, but I didn't want to be snared and exhibited."

"I saw *you,* you know." said Mrs. Boatright calmly, "or we wouldn't be here. Had nowhere to exhibit you, profitably, at the moment."

"You lay low?" The painter sighed. "Ships in the night. I am a vain man, amn't I? Well, let's see. Let's *see.*"

"The paper bag?" pressed Rosemary.

"Quiet, now," the painter's eyes roved. "Ah yes, the heart-shaped face. Saw *you.*"

"Me?" said Virginia.

"On the right side, well forward?"

"Yes."

"Where you could turn those gentle eyes where you liked," said the painter, mischievously.

Virginia's face turned a deep soft pink. Lee Coffey's ears stood up.

"I didn't try to see whether *he* was looking sly at your. Perhaps in the mirror?" said the painter and swung to the driver. "*Were* you?"

"Me!" exploded Lee, and then softly, "Me?"

"Theo," said Mrs. Boatright severely, "you are showing off again. And behaving like a bad little boy."

"I don't care to have her embarrassed," said the bus driver stiffly. "Get on to the subject, the poison."

The painter flapped both hands. "Don't mind me," he said irritably. "I see things. I can't help it." (The bus driver picked up the nurse's hand in his, although neither of them seemed aware of this or looked at each other.) The painter clasped his hands behind him and arched his thin ribcase and teetered on his toes. "There was that ear . . ."

"*Whose* ear?" demanded Rosemary fiercely.

"Can't say. All I noticed *was* the ear. We could advertise. Wait a minute . . . Didn't Mary Anne say your name is *Gibson?*"

"Yes."

"Then somebody spoke to you."

"Did they? Why, yes," said Mr. Gibson. "Yes, that's true. Somebody said my name, twice. Once while I waited. Once, just as I was getting off. *Somebody knew me.*" He was suddenly excited.

"Who, Kenneth? Who?"

He shook his head. "I . . . don't know," he said with shame. "I paid no attention."

"He was sunk," said the painter nodding vigorously, looking like a turkeycock, his wattles shaking. "He was *sunk*. I noticed that."

"Did you notice who spoke to him?" Rosemary demanded.

The painter looked dashed. "Darned if I did," he said with chagrin. "I'm so eye-minded. Oh, I heard. But I made no picture of the speaker. I did not connect. However . . ." He paused in vanity until all of them were waiting on him. "I believe I did see somebody pick up the paper bag."

"Who?"

"Who?"

"Who?"

They exploded like popcorn.

"A young woman. A mere girl. A very handsome young female," the painter said. "I was looking at her face. But I do believe she picked up that greenish paper bag and carried it off the bus. Yes."

"When?"

"After he got off, just after. I was driven back to the ear by default."

"Who was she?"

The painter shrugged. "I'd know her," he said, "but I'd have to see her. Names, labels, mean nothing to me."

"Where did she get off?"

"Oh, not many blocks after . . ." Distance meant nothing to him, either.

"Was she dark?" said Paul Townsend, tensely.

"I suppose you mean . . . to put it, crudely . . . was her hair of a darkish color? Yes."

"Jeanie! cried Paul. "Oh Lord, oh God, it could have been Jeanie. Where's your telephone?"

"No telephone," said Mrs. Boatright. "Who is Jeanie?"

Paul had moved into the center somehow. He was tall and angry. He glared at everyone. He was a raging lion.

"But Paul," said Rosemary, "what makes you think it could be Jeanie?"

"Because she went to her music lesson, just about *then*. Her teacher is out on the Boulevard. She *could* have got on as he got off. *She* knew him. *She* would have spoken. She *might* have taken his empty seat. Jeanie!" Paul's handsome face contorted.

"Who is Jeanie?" the painter wanted to know.

"My daughter!" yelled Paul. "My daughter!"

"But if Jeanie saw *him* . . ." Rosemary frowned and concentrated.

"How could she know where he'd been sitting? How could she know it was him," said Paul, losing control of his grammar in his agitation, "who left the poison? Maybe she . . . Oh, no!" Paul groaned. "Jeanie's got sense. Jeanie's a darned sensible kid. You all know that," he appealed pitifully. "But I got to call home. If anything's happened to Mama! Oh no, oh Lord . . . I've got to get to a phone. She was *pretty,* you say?"

The painter said, "She was lovely." His eyes were watching. "Not quite the same thing."

"Jeanie is lovely. That's sure. I'm getting out of here." Paul was beside himself. "Listen, Mama likes her supper early. Jeanie will be fixing Mama's supper too soon now. It's getting on to five o'clock. I got to call. If Mama were to get that poison, what would I do?"

"Mama?" Mrs. Boatright raised her brows at the Gibsons.

"His mother-in-law," said Rosemary rather awesomely. "An old lady . . . a crippled old lady . . ."

"She may be old but she's lived long enough to know something," raved Paul, as upset as anyone had ever seen him. "She's raised my Jeanie—raised *me*, if you want to know the truth. She's a wonderful old lady, God love her. . . . The whole house depends on her. I could *never* have gone on without her, when Frances died . . . Listen, I'm very sorry but I have to get going and it's my . . . well, my car."

"Mr. Marsh," said Rosemary, springing up, "could it possibly be his daughter?"

"Could be," said Theo Marsh. "No resemblance."

"Jeanie looks like her dead mother," cried Paul. "Not a bit like me. Listen, I'll take you all back into town, but you'll have to come *now*."

"I'll drive, said Lee Coffey with instant sympathy. "You're kinda upset and I'm faster. I suppose this is possible?" he said to the rest of them.

"Is there a phone at the junction?" cried Paul.

"Yes, a phone," said Virginia, her hand still in Lee's hand.

"Oh yes," said Theo Marsh, "at the gas station. *Up,*

Lavinia." The model stood up in her weird garb. The rest of them were streaming to the door.

"Wait for us," said the painter.

"Are *you* coming?" said the bus driver curiously.

"Certainly, *I'm* coming. If you think I'm not going to be on hand to see how this works out! I'm not a man who misses much. Snap it up, Lavinia. We dump her at the junction. Her father runs the gas station."

Mr. Gibson had time to marvel at this, as they streaked for the car.

Lee, Virginia, and Paul were in the front, as before. In the back, Mrs. Boatright's broad beam occupied the center solidly. On her left, Theo Marsh held Lavinia on his lap, and on the right, Mr. Gibson held his wife, Rosemary. He felt tumbled and breathless, but fallen into a warm and lovely place, in the lee of Mrs. Boatright's good and warm and solid flesh, with Rosemary's physical being pressing upon his thighs and his arm holding her.

The car flew down the hill. It stopped. Everybody swayed. Paul was out and at the telephone. Lavinia kicked the long blue skirt about with her bare feet and got out clumsily. Mr. Gibson heard her say, "Hi, Paw."

"I suggest you get some pants on," a man's voice said without passion, "and take over the pumps, Lavinia. Mother's been announcing dinner the last five minutes and I'm famished."

Mr. Gibson heard Paul shouting that the line was busy. That something terrible could have happened.

Theo Marsh bellowed back, "Look here, you at the telephone. Let Lavinia get on the telephone. She's absolutely reliable. I guarantee that." He was leaning over the side waving his long skinny arms.

"No nerves, Lavinia," said the unseen father complacently. "What's up?"

"Let *her* keep calling," bawled the artist. "While we get there."

"I'll tell them," said Lavinia. "Don't touch any olive oil and youse guys is on the way."

"No nerves, no diction," said the sad voice of the gas station man, with a shudder, unseen by but nevertheless divined by Mr. Gibson.

"Yes, do it." Paul was hoarse. "I can't stand here." He beat the telephone number out three times. (Lavinia got it the first time.) Then Paul climbed back into the car.

"All right, Lee," said Virginia to the bus driver.

"Off we go," howled the painter in joy. 'So long, Lavinia. Good girl," he told them. "She understands one hell of a lot about art."

"She does?" said Rosemary breathlessly. The car lurched and Mr. Gibson hung on to her.

Rosemary leaned to see around Mrs. Boatright. "Of course, as an artist, Mr. Marsh," she said in suspiciously sweet tones, "you live way out here to retreat from reality."

"The hell I retreat from reality," said the artist angrily. "Who told you that?" Mrs. Boatright contrived to shrink her bosom back against her backbone, somewhat, as they talked across her. " *I* see more reality in half a minute than any one of you can see in a day," raved the artist. "*I* don't even drive a car. I . . ."

"Because of your eyesight?" piped up Mr. Gibson promptly.

"Right," said Theo grumpily. "Good for you, Gibson, if it was Gibson speaking." The artist retreated into silence. Mr. Gibson felt as if he had just won a thrust.

"Hey?" said the bus driver over his shoulder. "What's this?"

"He sees too much," explained Mr. Gibson. "An ear, for instance. He'd be in the ditch."

"I bet he would." Rosemary actually chuckled in her old Rosemaryish way. Mr. Gibson was exhilarated. He pressed his cheek secretly against her sleeve, not wishing to laugh. After all, he was still a criminal. But with mirth rumbling inside of him, just the same.

"Pretty keen, this Gibson," said the bus driver to the blonde. "Mighty lively corpse he makes, hey?"

Paul said tensely, "Drive the car."

Virginia said soothingly, "He is. He will."

"Don't worry, Paul," said Rosemary, rather gaily. "Jeanie is a sensible girl."

"I know that." Paul turned and swept them with a harassed look. He put both palms swiftly over his hair, not quite holding his head, but smoothing it on, as he turned to yearn ahead once more.

"I've got the rest of you sorted out, but who *is* Paul?" asked the painter, reducing his volume. "*He* wasn't on the bus."

"He's a neighbor of theirs," said Mrs. Boatright. "This

is his car. We ought to have called the police, you know."

The painter said under his breath to the back seat, "I doubt very much it was *his* daughter who took the green paper bag. *She* was distinguished. Whereas he . . ." The painter made an unspellable noise. It meant Big Deal!

"Paul," said Rosemary rather drowsily, "is as good as he is beautiful."

"And perishing *dull*," said Marsh. "Am I right?"

Rosemary's arm came around Mr. Gibson's neck, to hang on, of course, for they were speeding. "Well, he *is* conventional," she said softly. "He's nice, but . . . everybody can't be interesting, like *you*." She leaned from Mr. Gibson's breast to peer at the painter.

"Oh ho, *I'm* interesting all right," said Theo Marsh.

Mr. Gibson felt furiously jealous. This conceited ass was seventy if he was a day.

"And deeply interested, too. Same thing, you realize. Say, what's-your-name-Gibson . . . why did you plan to kill yourself in the first place?" asked Theo Marsh. "No money?"

"Money!" shrieked Rosemary.

"Why not?" said the artist. "Money is something *I* take care to have about me. Believe me. I'm a shrewd moneymaker. Am I not, Mary Anne?"

"A leech and a bloodsucker." said Mrs. Boatright calmly.

"Well, money is a serious matter," said Theo with a pout, as if nobody would talk seriously. "So naturally, I wondered. Is he broke?"

"No," said Rosemary shortly.

"In some kind of way," said Lee Coffey, with his keen ears stretched backward, "he was broke . . ."

"I assume," said Theo Marsh loftily, "that *something* bothers him. Want to know what, that's all."

"He won't say," said Mrs. Boatright, "but perhaps he can't . . ."

"Yes, he can," said Theo Marsh. "He's articulate. And I'm listening. It interests me."

"Oh, it does?" said Mr. Gibson spitefully. He felt Rosemary's body tensing.

"Shall I guess?" said she, in a brave voice that was full of fear. "He married me ten weeks ago . . . to s-save me. He *likes* to help waifs and strays, you see. It's his hobby. But when I got well . . . there he was, still stuck with me."

"What!" cried Mr. Gibson, outraged. He grabbed her with both arms as if she might fall with his agitation. "No. No!"

"Well, then?" she trembled. "I don't know why you wanted to do it, Kenneth. I only guess . . . it's something Ethel put in your head." She leaned forward, far away from him, and put her hands on the front seat and laid her face on her forearm. "I'm afraid—it's something about me." And Mr. Gibson's heart ached terribly.

"We don't know," said Lee mournfully, over his shoulder. "Nope, we still don't know what it was that shook him."

Virginia said, "I should think you might tell us. We've been so close. Please tell us." Her little face was a moon setting on the horizon of the back of the seat. Her hand came up and touched Rosemary's hair compassionately. "It would be good for you to tell us."

Mrs. Boatright said with massive confidence. "He will, in a minute."

Paul said, "You can take a short cut up Appleby Place."

"I'm way ahead of you," said Lee, "and Lavinia's had them on the phone by now."

"Lavinia!" spat Paul. "That girl with no clothes!" He evidently couldn't imagine being *both* naked and reliable.

Marsh said airily in his high incisive voice, "I guess Gibson likes his secret reason; hugs it to his bosom. Won't show it to us. Oh, no, we might spoil his fun."

"Don't *talk* like that!" cried Rosemary, straightening up. "You sound like Ethel."

So everybody talked at once, telling the painter who Ethel was.

"An amateur," the painter groaned. He had one foot up against the seat ahead. His socks were yellow. "How I loathe and despise these amateurs! These leaping amateurs! *Amateur* critics." He uttered a long keen. "Amateur psychologists are among the worst. Skim a lot of stuff out of an abbreviated article in a twenty-five-cent magazine . . . and then they know. So they treat their friends and neighbors out of their profundity. They put their big fat clumsy hands in where the daintiest probe can't safely go, and they rip and they tear. Nothing so cruel as an amateur, doing good. I'd like to strangle the lot of them."

Mr. Gibson stirred. "No," he said. "No, now I want you

to be fair to Ethel. I'll have to try to make you understand. It's just that . . . perhaps Ethel made me see it . . . but it's the doom." There. He had told them.

"Doom?" said Mrs. Boatright encouragingly.

He would have to explain. "We aren't free," he said earnestly. "We are simply doomed. It . . . well, it just suddenly hit me very hard. To realize . . . I mean to believe and begin to apply—the fact that choice is only an illusion. That we are at the mercy of things *in ourselves* that we cannot even know. That we are not able to help ourselves or each other . . ."

They were all silent, so he pressed on.

"We are dupes, puppets. What each of us will do can be predicted. Just as the bomb . . . for instance . . . is bound to fall, human nature being what it . . ."

"Baloney," groaned the painter. "The old sad baloney! Predict *me*—Gibson. I dare you! You mean to say you got yourself believing that old-fashioned drivel?" he sputtered out.

But Rosemary said, "Yes, I see. Yes, I know. Me, too."

Then everybody else in the car, except Paul, seemed to be talking at once.

The bus driver's voice emerged on top. "Lookit!" he shouted. "You cannot, *from where you sit,* predict! I told you. Accidents! There's the whole big fat mixed-up universe . . ."

"What if *I* can't predict?" said Mr. Gibson, somewhat spiritedly defending his position. "An expert . . ."

"No, no. We are *all* ignorant," cried the nurse. "But it's the experts who *know* that. They know we're guessing. They know we're guessing better and better, because *they're* trying to check up on the guesses. You *have* to believe that, Mr. Gibson."

Mr. Gibson was suddenly touched. His heart quivered as if something had reached in and touched it.

Mrs. Boatright cleared her throat. "Organized human effort," she began.

"This is *not* the PTA, Mary Anne," the artist said severely. "This is one simple intelligent male. Give me a crack at him." He had come so far forward to peer at Mr. Gibson that he seemed to be crouching, angular as a cricket, on air. "Listen, Gibson. Take a cave man."

"Yes," said Mr. Gibson, helplessly, with a kind of melting feeling. "I'm taking one."

"Did he foresee his descendants flying over the North Pole to get from here to Europe tomorrow?"

"Of course not."

"So . . . how can *you* be as narrow-minded as a cave man?"

"Narrow?"

"Certainly. You extrapolate a future on what's known now. You extend the old lines. What you don't take into account are the surprises."

"Hey!" said the bus driver. "Hey! Hey!"

"Every big jump is a surprise, a revelation," lectured the artist, "and a tangent off the old. Penicillin. Atom splitting. Who guessed they were coming?"

"Exactly," cried Virginia. "Or the wheel? Or television? How do we know what's coming next?" She was all excited. "Maybe some whole vast opening up in a direction we've hardly thought of . . ."

"Good girl," said Theo Marsh. "Have you ever done any modeling?"

"Of the spirit, too," boomed Mrs. Boatright. "Of the mind. Men *have* developed ideals undreamed in antiquity. You simply cannot deny it. Would your cave man understand the Red Cross?"

"Or the S.P.C.A.," said the bus driver, "him and his saber-toothed playmates. Doom—schmoom. Also, if you *gotta*, you very often do. Take a jump, I mean. I'm talking about the bomb . . ."

"So the bomb might not fall," said Rosemary. She lifted her clasped hands in a kind of ecstasy, "because men might find something even better than common sense by tomorrow morning. Who knows? Not Ethel! Ethel is too—"

"Too rigid, I expect," said the painter. "Death is too rigid. Rigor is mortis. Keep your eyes open. You'll be surprised!" This was his credo. Mr. Gibson found himself stretching the physical muscles around his eyes.

"It's gonna fall if you sit on your fanny and expect it," the bus driver said, "that's for sure. But everybody isn't just sitting around, telling themselves *they* are so smart *they* can see their fate coming. Lookit, we'll know the latest news today, when we look backward from fifty years. Not before. The present views with alarm. It worries. It should. But these trends sneak up like a mist that you don't notice."

"Righto!" shouted the artist. "*You* don't even see what's already around you in your own home town."

"People can, too, help each other," said Rosemary. She was sitting on his lap yet turned in facing him. "And I'm the living *proof*. You helped me because you *wanted* to, Kenneth. There *wasn't* any other reason."

"The ayes have it," the painter said. (Perhaps he said "eyes.") "You are overruled, Gibson. You haven't got a leg to die on. You can't logically kill yourself on that silly old premise." He drew back upon the seat and crossed his legs complacently.

The bus driver said dubiously, "However, logic . . ."

The nurse suddenly put her forehead against his arm.

Mrs. Boatright said firmly, "If you see that you were wrong, now you *must* admit it. That is the *only* way to progress."

And then they waited.

Mr. Gibson's churning mind settled, sad and slow as a feather. "But in my error," he said quietly, "I may have caused a death."

Paul said uncontrollably, "If anything happened to Mama or Jeanie, I'll never forgive you."

"Don't say 'never,' " said Virginia, raising her head and speaking gently.

"It ain't scientific to say 'never,' hey?" said the bus driver, and leaned and kissed her ear.

The car shot off the boulevard upon a short cut.

Everyone was silent. The excitement was over. The poison was still lost. They hadn't found it.

And if in error there was learning and if in blame there was responsibility and if in ignorance there was hope—and if in life there are surprises—and if in doom there were these cracks—still, they had not put their hands upon a little bottle full of death, and innocently labeled olive oil. And *it* was no illusion.

Chapter XIX

MR. GIBSON sat holding his wife in his lap, and this was bitter-sweet. "Rosemary," he said softly in a moment, almost whispering, "why did you say you hadn't run the needle into your finger . . . when you had?"

"Why do I *think* I said it?" But her face softened and she discarded the bitterness. "I just didn't care to have Ethel know . . ." Her breath was on his forehead.

"Know what, mouse?"

"How much," said Rosemary. She drew a little away to look down into his eyes. "I loved our cottage," she said. "My—sentiments. She hasn't any sympathy with sentiment. I suppose it was sentimental, but I didn't want to go away."

Mr. Gibson squeezed his own eyes shut.

"But *you* went away, Kenneth. Ever since the accident," she whispered into his hair. "What did Ethel say to you?" He hid his face against where her heart was beating. "I thought maybe you agreed," she said, "with *her* that I tried to be rid of my bargain. You would have been kind to me, even so. I couldn't tell."

"That was an accident," he murmured. "Mouse, I told you . . ."

"I told *you* things . . . you didn't seem to believe," she said. "She *is* your sister, you *do* respect her. I thought you believed her, and you *said* you couldn't remember—I was afraid. . . . She had me so confused."

Paul said loudly, "Turn right, here. That's it. The third driveway." Paul, who was single-minded now. Paul, who said "Don't worry" when everyone did. But who urged them to worry when they seemed not to. Paul—who was so young—under whose genial good manners lurked a rather sulky boy.

"Ethel will be there now, I guess," said Rosemary, sucking in breath.

She moved, increasing the distance between them. The car stopped. Mr. Gibson opened his eyes. He saw the little cottage's roof on his left with its vines. It looked like home. But home was not for him . . . not any more. He had been confused and in hopeless confusion, he sadly surmised, he had doomed himself.

He limped badly, getting up on Paul's front terrace.

Jeanie Townsend, alive and strong, opened the door and cried eagerly, "Oh, did you find it?"

"She's not the one," croaked Theo Marsh. "I didn't think so."

Paul grabbed her in both his arms. "I was so scared, baby," he panted. "I thought maybe you'd got on the same bus . . . I thought maybe you had that poison."

"Oh, for Heaven's sakes, Daddy!" Jeanie wiggled indignantly to get away from him. "How dumb do you think I am?"

"How's Mama?" Paul let her go and rushed past her. Obviously, there was no poison here.

Jeanie looked at the crew of them . . . half a dozen suddenly drooping people on the doorstep. "Won't you come in?" she snapped, the polite child struggling with the angry one.

"Did Lavinia call?" asked Lee Coffey. "Hey, Jeanie?" He had exactly the same air with the young girl as he had with the elders.

"Somebody called. Was that Lavinia? We knew already. It was on the radio." Jeanie tossed her cropped head. She had on a red skirt and white blouse and a little red latticework on her bare feet for shoes. "When I went down to the mailbox—oh, a long time ago—I heard it on Miss Gibson's radio. So I turned on ours." She looked very haughty as if of course she would know what was going on in the world.

Mr. Gibson looked at Rosemary and she at him. "Then Ethel knows," he murmured. He could not see an inch into the future. Rosemary moved until their shoulders touched.

"Well, I guess she mightn't know it was you," said Jeanie, backing inward, "because it didn't give your name on the radio. Grandma guessed that part of it."

"And you didn't run over and tell this Ethel or hash it out with her, neighborly? Hey?" asked the bus driver curiously.

"No," said Jeanie. She looked a little troubled about this but she didn't rationalize an excuse. Obviously she hadn't felt like hashing things out with Ethel Gibson. "Aren't you all coming in?"

They all came in.

Paul was in the living room and down on his knees beside old Mrs. Pyne's chair, and his handsome head was bowed. It was a strange position for him . . . theatrical, corny.

Mrs. Pyne was saying, as to a child, "But Paul, dear, you needn't have had a moment's worry about Jeanie or me . . ."

Paul said, "You'll never know . . ." He sounded like a big ham.

Jeanie's eyes flashed. "What makes you think I'd eat any old food I found lying around or feed it to Grandma? Don't you think I know better? Honestly, Daddy!"

But Paul knelt there.

Now Mrs. Pyne smile around at them all, and her smile plucked out Mr. Gibson. "I'm so glad to see you," said the old lady. "I've been praying for you constantly since last I saw you."

Mr. Gibson moved toward her and took her frail dry hand. It had strength in it. He wanted to thank her for her prayers, but it seemed awkward, like applauding in church. She was a perfect stranger to him, anyhow, now that he saw her as the core of this house.

"Say, excuse me," said Theo Marsh, in a businesslike way, "are you interested in modeling?" Mrs. Pyne looked astonished.

"My name is Helen Pyne," said the old lady with spunk in her voice. "Who are you, sir?"

"Theodore Marsh, a humble painter." This Theo was part clown. He made a leg. "Always looking for good faces."

"Humble, hey?" murmured the bus driver comically. "I'm Lee Coffey. I drive the bus."

"I'm Virginia Severson. I was a passenger."

"I am Mrs. Walter Boatright," said that lady, as if this sufficed. She stood, like the speaker of the evening, thoughtfully organizing her notes in her mind.

But it was Rosemary who burst out to Theo Marsh . . . "If it wasn't Jeanie you saw . . . then we don't know . . ."

"It wasn't Jeanie," said the artist. He had cocked his head as if to see Mrs. Pyne upside down. Mr. Gibson suffered an enlargement. He, too, saw the old lady's face, the sweetness around the eyes, the firmness of her dainty chin. Mrs. Pyne was not only more beautiful, she was even prettier than Jeanie.

"Then who? Then who?" Rosemary implored.

"I have great confidence in the police department," said Mrs. Boatright decisively, and took a throne. Rosemary stared at her and ran for the telephone.

Paul came out of his trance or prayer or whatever it was. "How did you know so much about what was going on?" he asked his mother-in-law adoringly.

"I knew it was bad, of course," the old lady said soberly, "when I heard Rosemary call. When Jean turned on the

adio, I knew at once who had left the bottle on the bus.
had just seen such trouble in his face, you know. Although
here was nothing I could do."

"Mrs. Pyne," said Mr. Gibson impulsively, "what you
said made it impossible. I don't think I would have done
t. But, of course, by then the trouble was different. I had
already lost the poison."

"And haven't found it," she said sadly.

"No." He met her eyes. He accepted his guilt and her
mercy.

"We must all pray," said Mrs. Pyne.

"Trouble?" said the bus driver. His eyes slewed around
to Virginia. "Trouble and logic . . . how do they jibe? I
don't think we got to the bot—"

Virginia seemed to shush him.

Rosemary wailed on the phone, "Nothing? Nothing at
all?" She hung it up. She walked back toward them.
"Nothing. No news of it at all," she said and twisted her
hands.

"No news is good news," said Paul.

But they all looked around at each other.

"A dead end, hey?" said the bus driver. "Ring around
a rosy and no place to go from here." Fumes of energy
boiled out of him and curled back with no place to go.

"Think!" said Virginia fiercely. "*I'm* trying to think.
Think, Mrs. Boatright." The little nurse shut her eyes.

Mrs. Boatright shut her eyes but her lips moved. Mr.
Gibson realized that Mrs. Walter Boatright was importuning
a superior in heaven, on his account.

But they had come to an end. There was no place else
to go.

He had rocked to his own feet now. It was time he took
over. He said vigorously, "You have all done so much. You
have done wonders. You must all go about your business,
now, with my grat—my love," he said loudly. "It's on
God's knees . . . I guess, after all." (Was this the same as
doom, he wondered?) "Rosemary and I must go across to
Ethel." This was his duty.

"Yes," Rosemary agreed somberly.

"Ethel's hard by *here?*" said Theo Marsh with a wicked
gleam in his eye.

"Theo," said Mrs. Boatright warningly.

Paul Townsend was himself again, and host in this

house. "How about a drink first?" he said cordially. "I
think we need one. Don't worry, Gibson . . ." He stopped
himself cold.

"Wurra, wurra," said the bus driver. "Each for his own.
That's what makes the mare go." He took a gloomy bite
of his thumbnail.

Paul said, "I guess I dragged you all here for nothing."
He looked boyishly penitent.

"A little drink won't do me any harm," said Lee. "Virginia would like one, too."

Theo Marsh perched like a restless bird on the edge of
a table. "Thirsty as the desert in August, myself," he admitted. "What's to do now?" He cracked a knuckle.

Mrs. Boatright said, "We don't seem to have any clear
course of procedure." She assembled her will. "I will call
home and have a car sent, to take any of you wherever you
wish. But first I would enjoy a rather weak drink, Paul.
Thank you. Meantime, we may think of something." Mrs.
Boatright was not accustomed to being beaten by circum-
stance.

Jeanie said, "I'll help you tend bar, Dad." And the bus
driver began to tell Mrs. Pyne the saga of their search.

It was curiously like a party, and a party of loosened
tongues, at that, well past the polite preliminaries. Mr.
Gibson sat beside Rosemary on a sofa and tried to remember that he was a criminal. Somebody, somewhere, could
be dead, or now dying, by his hand.

Young Jeanie seemed to have caught on to the wide-open
atmosphere. Holding the tray, she said to the Gibsons,
"I'm sorry I got so mad, but Dad should have trusted me.
My goodness, most of the time he leans on me too much."

"He's so fond of you, dear," said Rosemary, "and of
your grandmother, too."

"He's absolutely tied to Grandma's apron strings," said
Jeanie impatiently. "I *wish* he'd get married."

"*Do* you?" said Rosemary sharply.

"Of course, we both do. Don't we, Grandma?"

"Wish Paul would marry?" Mrs. Pyne sighed. "We've
not been very successful matchmakers."

"Look, I'm happy," said Paul, passing drinks.

Rosemary leaned forward and said deliberately, "But
Mrs. Pyne, wouldn't Jeanie be terribly jealous of a step-
mother? Isn't a teen-age daughter bound to be?"

"Subconsciously?" said Virginia, her clean-cut little mouth forming the word with distaste.

Mr. Gibson felt very queer. He kept his face a blank. He had a conviction that Lee Coffey, Theo Marsh, all of them, could see right through his skin.

"Here comes Ethel, hey?" said Lee. "Oh boy, this Ethel—"

"Jeanie," said Mrs. Pyne gently, "is *truly* fond of Paul."

"Honestly!" burst Jeanie. "How can she think that about *me?* She doesn't even know me. And I know the facts of life! I've been trying to marry Dad off for four years now. Pretty consciously," she flared.

"Ethel though," said the bus driver comfortably, *"she* knows better. Hey, Rosemary?" He winked.

"I don't think she knows much about teen-agers," said Jeanie. "We're a pretty bright bunch."

"Quite so," said Mrs. Boatright. "One should make a practice of listening to young people. Go on, my dear."

"We've even heard of Oedipus," Jeanie rushed on— flashing Mrs. Boatright a look of fierce response. "We're not stupid. I ask you, what's going to happen to Dad when I go off? And I'm *going,* some day."

"And I," said Mrs. Pyne, nodding calmly.

"If he hasn't got *somebody,* he's going to be just lost," said Jeanie. "He's an awful comfort-loving man."

Paul said, "These women . . . they nag me . . ." He lifted his glass. His eyes were suddenly inscrutable.

Mr. Gibson sipped his own drink, in automatic imitation. It was cold and tasteless, and then suddenly delicious.

"Well, of course," said Rosemary wickedly, "Ethel has her own ideas about crippled old ladies, too, Mrs. Pyne."

Paul looked very angry.

Mrs. Pyne lifted her hand, as if to forestall his anger and she smiled. "Poor Ethel," she said. "Well, she must live as best she can and think what will comfort her, I suppose. Never married. No children. Such a limited experience of life."

Mr. Gibson murmured his astonishment. "Ethel? Limited?" He had never thought of this.

"I don't think she has many connections with real people," said Mrs. Pyne. "That is to say, individuals. Or how could she judge them in such lumps?"

"She doesn't look—can't see," said Theo Marsh.

"They're a wild and wonderful lot," said the bus driver patting Virginia's hand, "if you take them one by one. And that's the way I like them." Virginia blushed and shushed him.

"Still," said Mr. Gibson, clearing his throat, "Ethel has had quite a successful business career. She has faced up to facts all her life." (His tongue felt loose. He was almost enjoying this party.) "Whereas I," he went on, "am the one who has had the limited existence. A little poetry. Some academic backwaters. Even in the war, I . . ."

"How can you read poetry and not notice the universe?" said Lee indignantly. "You know who is limited? Fella who reads nothing but the newspaper, watches nothing but his own p's and q's, plus TV in the evening, works for nothing but money, buys nothing with the money but a car or a steak, does what he *thinks* the neighbors do and don't notice the universe. Actually," he sank back and slipped his fingers on his glass, "I never met anybody like that, myself."

"You read about him in the newspaper," said Theo Marsh.

"What war, Mr. Gibson?" asked Virginia.

"Oh . . . both wars. I was too old for Korea . . ."

"Oh yes," said Rosemary with charming sarcasm. "He has had so little experience. Only two wars, you see. Then there was the depression, the years when he took care of his mother, when he paid for Ethel's education. And that was weak and drifting of him, wasn't it? The years he has taught . . . who counts those? Ethel doesn't. I don't see why not," she added in a low voice. "Or why, when a man has led a useful life for fifty-five years and is kind and generous and good . . . why Ethel seems to assume he is so naïve and so . . ."

"Innocent?" supplied Mr. Gibson, his eyes crinkling. (He was having a *lovely* time.)

"*Back*waters?" snapped Theo Marsh. "What d'ya mean? What does she think life is made of? Your name in the metropolitan newspapers? Café society?"

"No, no. Facts," said Mr. Gibson. "Mean-ness. People who run knives in your back. Egos and burglars . . ."

"Please." The painter stopped him with a loud groaning. "Why is everything loathsome and unpleasant called a fact? Thought fact was another name for truth. And evil truths may be . . . but truth does not *equal* evil. I'll tell you,

you can't paint a decent picture without the truth in it."

"Or write a decent poem, either," said the bus driver, "or teach a decent lesson. Or earn an honest penny. You know, I think he *is* innocent." He looked around belligerently.

"I think he's a dear," said Virginia warmly.

Mrs. Boatright was nodding judiciously. "Theo," said she, "I believe the Tuesday Club would listen to you on this subject . . ."

"For a hundred and fifty lousy bucks?" said Theo. "Bah! Those cheapskates!"

Mr. Gibson tried very hard not to be having so much fun. Here, beside Rosemary, in this clean and comfortable and charming room where the dainty gentlewoman in her wheel chair was their true hostess, where all these lively people spoke their minds . . . No, no—he *must* remember that he had to face the music.

Sometimes, however, he thought with a boom of pleasure that would not be denied, there *is* music. That's the funny thing! This group of people, the way they talked to him, the way they argued with him, contradicted him, tried to buck him up, liked him and worried for him, and fought with him against fate, and gave him of their own faiths . . . this touched him and made music in his heart. He thought no man had ever had so delightful an experience as he had had this day of his suicide.

But such pleasure was only stolen. He must go. He must face whatever would come, nor would it be music, altogether.

Chapter XX

HE STARTED TO RISE.

"Wait a minute," said the bus driver. "Listen, kids . . ."

"Yes, Lee?" said Mrs. Boatright alertly.

"We got our hair down, all of us. Hey? Let's not skim the surface here. Don't go, Gibson. Yet. *I* want to know the answer to one question that's been worrying me. Rosemary . . ."

"Yes, Lee?"

Mr. Gibson sat down. He trembled. This bus driver *wa* a shrewd man, in his own way.

"Now, this Ethel, she decides your subconscious want: to get rid of him. That's right, isn't it? Tell me, wha: reason did she decide your subconscious had for this?"

Rosemary flushed.

"She'd figured *out* a reason?"

"Yes," said Rosemary. "Of course she had." Her finger: turned her glass. "These marriages never work, you know," said Rosemary almost dreamily. "Kenneth is twenty-three years older than I. Isn't that terrible! Ethel thinks that subconsciously . . ." she went on very quiet and yet defian: and brave, "I *must* wish I had a younger mate."

"Like who? Hey?" said the bus driver, his eyes lively, his sandy lashes alert. The painter sat up. Mrs. Boatright looked suddenly very bland and supercalm.

"Like Paul," said Rosemary.

"Now we're getting to the bottom," said the bus driver with satisfaction.

"Aha!" said the painter.

"Oh now, look, Rosie," said Paul, crimson. "Now you know . . ."

"I *thought* I knew," said Rosemary, and smiled at him.

"If our hair is down," said Jeanie bluntly, "all right. I'll tell you something. *She* is too *old*—for Daddy."

Mr. Gibson felt a wave of shock ripple through him. Rosemary! Too old!

"He likes them rather plump, about five years older, and two inches shorter, than me," said Jeanie impudently, "as far as I can figure on the basis of experiments, so far."

"Now you . . . just be quiet, please," said Paul, much embarrassed. "I'm sorry, Rosie, but after all you *are* his wife. I certainly . . ."

"Don't be sorry," said Rosemary gently. Her face became very serene as she lifted it. "You've been kind, Paul. You've tried to comfort me. You've told me not to worry. But I am too old for you, of course. Just as you are . . . forgive me, dear Paul . . . just a bit too dull for my taste. You see, *I* like a seasoned man."

"Good for you," said Theo Marsh complacently. "Intelligent woman."

"Ethel just can't seem to believe," said Rosemary, calm

and sad, "anything so simple. The fact is, I *married* the man I love."

Mr. Gibson, looking at his glass, could see her fingers, slim and fair, upon her own.

"However," said Mr. Gibson out of a trance, able to speak quite coolly, although somewhat jerkily, "it is still possible that, as Ethel says, I am, for Rosemary, a father-image."

Rosemary looked at him with mild astonishment. "Not *my* father," she said calmly. "*My* father, since the day I was born, was mean and didactic and unjust and petty and spoiled and childish. I don't like to sound disloyal, but that's the truth. Kenneth isn't *anything* like *my* father," she explained graciously to them all.

"It is a little ridiculous, though," said Mr. Gibson chattily. (This was the strangest party!) "I am fifty-five years old, you see. For *me* to be so deep in love, for the first time in my life, is quite . . . comical. Somehow. It makes everybody smile."

"Smile?" said Virginia. "But of course! It's *nice!* It's pleasant to see."

"I should have said . . . snicker," revised Mr. Gibson.

"Who," growled the bus driver, "does it make snicker?"

"Not at all," said the artist. "*I* was in love last winter. If anyone had snickered at me, I'd have spit in their eye." He would have. Everyone believed this.

"How come this Ethel put the Indian sign on the both of you?" asked the bus driver. "How come she shook you? Anybody can see you two are in love." He was a gentle ruthless man.

"I was a rabbit," said Rosemary. "I should have spit in her eye." She was sitting very straight. "I am to blame."

Mr. Gibson felt exhausted and also very peaceful. "I, too," he said. "But I am old, lame, unsure . . . and extremely stupid. I permitted her to upset me. My fault. My blame." He wanted to cry. He drank thirstily.

"Whereas, our Paul," said the painter, "is as handsome as the hero in a slick magazine. And as good as he is beautiful. No offense. No offense. Sex, I presume?" He crossed his yellow socks and tried to look innocent. "According to lethal Ethel?"

"Lethal Ethel, that's *good,*" said the bus driver angrily. "That's *apt,* that is."

Virginia said, "Surely people *know* when they're in love
. . ." and bit her lips.

Rosemary leaned back with a little smile gentle on her
face. "Do you know something? There is a fact they never
take account of—in a magazine story or the movies either
. . . that *I* ever saw. Why is it you . . . want to be where
someone is? Why?" She looked at Virginia. "It *can't* be just
because he's good-looking. (Although Kenneth *is,* very.) It
certainly can't be just because somebody is *young.* To me,"
she continued to the lamp beside the sofa, "the most important thing of all is how much fun you have together,
and I don't mean sex. Although—" Rosemary gulped and
went on. "Do you understand me? I mean—just enjoying
each other's company. We had such good times . . . as I
had never known. We laughed," said Rosemary. She leaned
forward with sudden vehemence. "Why don't people talk
about *that* as if it were attractive? It is. It's powerfully attractive. I think it's the most powerful attraction of all."

"The most permanent," said Mrs. Pyne, softly.

"Absolutely," said Mrs. Boatright. "Or the race could
not endure. *All* beloved wives, for instance, are not size
twelve." She rocked a little indignantly on her great
haunches.

"Hm," said the artist, "my fourth wife now . . . I had
a most delightful companionship with that one, all around
the clock. And although her ankles were *not* perfect, she is
the one I mourn . . . it's a fact." He looked mildly astonished.

"I . . . agree," breathed Virginia. The bus driver slid
his eyes under his lashes.

Mr. Gibson, with joy shooting in his veins . . . and shame
and sorrow, too, but with an iron resolve that the rest of
this was his own private business however much he loved
—Yes, he did!—all of them . . . took Rosemary's hand and
got to his feet. He said with a simplicity that achieved
privacy with one stroke, "Thank you all very much for
everything you have done and said. But we must go now."

To Mrs. Pyne he said, "If you will pray for us—that
the poison be found . . ."

"I will," she vowed.

Paul said shyly, nervously, "Sure hope it works out O.K."

Jeanie said, "Oh, we all hope so!"

Mrs. Boatright said, "The police may still find it. Mustn't
underestimate the organization."

The painter said, "It could be on a dump heap, right now and you will *never* know . . . *never* hear . . . You realize?"

The nurse said, "Oh, please . . . be happy." Her whole cool responsible little person was dissolving in sentimental tears.

The bus driver said earnestly, "Lots of good books been written in jail; I mean to say, 'Stone walls do not . . .' "

"I'll remember that, Lee," said Mr. Gibson affectionately. For this man was the one who had set the fashion, the one who had decreed, in the beginning, that there would be no candy. He offered none now, really.

Mr. Gibson slipped one arm around Rosemary's waist and guided her out of the house.

They left seven people.

"He's a darling," sobbed Virginia. "She's a dear. . . . Can't we save them? *Think,* everybody!"

Then the seven were silent in that room—silent and sad and still fighting.

Mr. Gibson and his wife, Rosemary, walked rather slowly and quite silently along the terrace to its end and down the steps and across the double driveway. It was a quarter of six o'clock. A sweet evening coming. They passed the shining garbage cans. Beyond the steps to the kitchen there grew a shrub, and Mr. Gibson pulled his wife gently to the far side of this friendly green mass where no window overlooked them.

He took her in his arms and she came close. He kissed her gently and then again, less so. Her head came upon his shoulder.

"You do remember the restaurant, Kenneth?"

"I do. I do."

"How we laughed! I thought after you were hurt, that you couldn't, didn't remember."

But remembered woe was far away. She only sighed.

"I remember the fog, too," he murmured. "We said it was beautiful."

"We didn't—altogether—mean the fog?"

"No." He kissed her, once more, most tenderly. "It's an old-fashioned plot, mouse. Isn't it? A misunderstanding. But then, I am an old-fashioned man."

"I love you so," said Rosemary. "No matter what—don't leave me."

"No matter what," he promised. He was a criminal. He

might leave her, although not "really." There was bitter.
There was sweet.

In a few minutes, he turned her gently, and they began
to go up the steps to the kitchen door.

Chapter XXI

ETHEL GIBSON returned to the cottage shortly after four
o'clock that afternoon. She frowned to find the doors
unlocked, the place wide open, and empty. Very careless
of her brother! Still, he might be over at the Townsends',
just across the driveways. Ethel did not feel in a mood to
join him, if so. She had arranged her day in her mind and
did not like to break her plan with idle and unexpected
sociability.

She put off her summer suit-jacket and marched into the
kitchen. What disarray! Really, order was essential in so
small a house. Ethel did not like living in this cottage; an
apartment would be so much less labor. She thought they
would be moving elsewhere before very long. Now she
compressed her lips. Lettuce limpening on the open counter.
Bread not neatly in the bread box. Cocoa, tea, should be
on the shelves. Cheese ought to be refrigerated. A green
paper bag. Now what was this? A tiny bottle of olive oil.
Imported! *Much* too expensive!

She shook her head and proceeded to clear the things
away, properly washed the lettuce and put it in the crisping
bin, the cheese in the icebox, threw the paper bag into the
kitchen wastebasket, placed cans and bottles in the cupboard.

She stepped into the living room long enough to switch
on the radio. Music was a habit with her. She paid no attention to it but felt its absence.

She then walked back to her (and Rosemary's) bedroom,
drew off her business clothes and hung them, put on a
cotton dress. Ethel then threw herself down upon the bed
to relax. Music came distantly. When there were voices,
she did not listen. She never listened to commercials. Her
mind ran over the first day at this office. This job would
serve. She already felt that she had some clues to the hid-

den springs of the boss's character. She foresaw an orderly, courageous, and useful life in this quiet town. Excellent for her health. She dozed.

She was wakened at a quarter after five by the telephone. The house was still empty.

"Yes?"

"This is the Townsend Laboratories calling," said a female voice. "Is Mr. Kenneth Gibson there?"

"No, he is not." Ethel was crisp.

"Where is he, do you know?"

"No, I do not. I daresay he will be here at dinner time."

"When?" The voice faded feebly.

"At a quarter of six."

"Oh. Well, will you be sure to have him call this number?"

Ethel took down the number.

"It's important," said the voice, fading again as if in some mysterious agitation.

"I'll tell him," said Ethel, soothingly.

Ethel hung up. She was slightly annoyed.

Inconsiderate! Consideration was the first rule in such a ménage as this. Rosemary should have returned, must soon. Where could Ken be? She couldn't imagine. Yes, she could. Probably he was lost in a book at the branch library.

Dinner at a quarter of six.

She would start dinner.

They knew the dinner hour.

The radio still played. She felt a bit martyred in this mysterious loneliness and she turned it off, feeding a grievance.

She went into the kitchen and began to prepare their dinner. It would be very simple. Ethel approved of a spaghetti dinner, inexpensive and nourishing and easy to put together—these packaged brands. She dumped the boughten sauce out into a pan. Thought better of this. One ought to doctor up a boughten sauce, she knew. Ethel chopped an onion fine and put it into the sauce. She was not a sensitive cook. She had eaten what restaurants put before her, for so many years. Food was food. It was either cheap or it was expensive. Still, she realized that she ought to have sautéed the onions. Perhaps in the olive oil? What did Ken mean it for, anyway? The bottle didn't hold enough for a salad dressing. Ethel did not like it in a dressing, having made do with cheap vegetable oils for so

long. Surely not for fruit! No, he must have fancied the
taste of olive oil in the spaghetti sauce. Perhaps it was
some fancy of Rosemary's.

She grimaced but took the bottle down and turned the
cap. Oh, well . . . she dumped it into the saucepan. She
hoped it would not taste too much. She washed out the
bottle and set it upside down to drain. King Roberto stood
on his head. Ethel filled a large pot with water for the
pasta.

She began to cut up fruit for salad. She doubted the
lettuce would be crisp at all. Five thirty-four and nobody
home *yet*.

Ethel began to set the table in the dining alcove of the
living room. From here she could see the driveways and
she heard and saw Paul's car come in and a great load
of people begin to get hastily out of it. Ethel averted her
eyes. It was beneath her to spy on the neighbors. A
party, she presumed. The word "party" meant something
lightweight to her, timewasting, profitless chitchat. (Nobody ever asked Ethel to parties.)

Now the table was set. The water at a boil. The sauce
ready enough. She turned it low. She mixed the salad.

When the clock said twenty of six, Ethel felt injured.
She threw the pasta into the boiling water, and went into
the living room and sat down with her back to the mantel
to watch the clock on the opposite wall.

She would knit for nine minutes.

Then dinner would be ready. And they *should* remember and be considerate. *She* was always considerate.

At eleven minutes of six she marched to the kitchen.
She heard their feet.

"Where on earth have you been?" said Ethel heartily.
"I see you're together . . ."

"Yes," said Mr. Gibson, "we are together." He was a
little surprised to see the same old Ethel, standing on both
feet in her accustomed way, vigorous and sure of herself.

"Dinner is *exactly* ready," said Ethel ."Now, you just
have time to wash. There is nothing for you to do, Rosemary. I've done it all. Now, get to the table while I drain
this and mix in the sauce. Shoo!" said Ethel, indulgently.

Meekly, they crossed the kitchen. But they kissed in the
hall.

"Doesn't know . . ." said Mr. Gibson wonderingly.

"No, she doesn't seem to. They aren't broadcasting your name . . ."

"Well, we must tell—"

"Yes . . ."

"Not easy."

"No." The sweet was so very sweet.

"Everybody ready?" hallooed Ethel.

Mr. Gibson let Rosemary go and he went into his own place. It already looked antique to him, a former way of life. Could he have books in a cell, he wondered? Alas, he couldn't have Rosemary. Face reality. Face wicked folly. Face love. Face it, that you are beloved.

He washed, musing, perceiving that Ethel was right. Or somewhat right. He had *not* seen clearly his own motives. He *had* rationalized. He had plastered a black philosophy in the mind over a quivering wound in the heart. Although it was not really that simple, either. Still, worms *might* have eaten him. . . . Well, he knew a little more now. He knew he had been too suggestible, too quick to abandon his own faiths. He ought to have trusted himself better.

Ethel made us both doubt ourselves, he mused, gave us that terrible feeling that one *cannot* trust oneself, no use to try. Such doubt as this, in quantity, judiciously used, might be a tonic and a medicine. But oh, too much, swallowed blindly at a bad time, had shaken him to his foundations.

It was dangerous stuff.

He met Rosemary in the hall. Their hands touched. They went across the living room to the dining alcove.

"Sit ye doon," said Ethel with ponderous good will and forbearance. "You naughty children." Her eyes were wise and speculating. She'd soon "know" where they had been.

They sat them down. Ethel spooned portions of spaghetti from the steaming mass in the wooden bowl. "Confess," she said. "What have you been up to?"

"There was a little mixup," said Mr. Gibson. He stared at the spaghetti, not feeling any appetite.

Rosemary nervously took up her fork. "We'll tell you about it, as best we can," she began. Dear Rosemary, brave enough to try to help him tell.

"I suppose you've had a talk?" said Ethel, giving them one of her looks. "Now, my dears, it is not my business and I do not pry. It is your privilege to have your little secrets—"

Rosemary put the fork down abruptly.

"Any decision that will affect me," said Ethel kindly, "I'm sure you will tell me about."

"Yes," said Rosemary steadily.

Mr. Gibson saw, in Ethel's eyes, himself, the lamb, the softhearted, the unworldly, the born bachelor, wifeless, living on into old age with his devoted spinster sister. Doomed to this. It was not true.

"We are very much in love, Ethel," he said quietly and firmly, "Rosemary and I."

Ethel's eyeballs swiveled and a blank look came down. But her mouth twitched in tiny disbelief, and the veiled eyes wondered. She did not speak.

But Rosemary spoke, "Just what was said—"

"What . . . ?"

"Just what was said. That's what is *meant*, Ethel."

"I'm so very glad," said Ethel in a false-sounding flutter. "But don't let dinner get cold . . ."

She didn't believe them. Her face remained blank but Mr. Gibson had an image of her thoughts, writhing and scrambling to detect some "real" meaning behind what he had said . . . until they writhed like . . . like a bowl of spaghetti. He couldn't stomach the stuff. However, he had better eat her dinner or offend her. He turned his fork.

Ethel's fork thrust into her spaghetti.

Suddenly, people were shouting. Startled, they all looked toward the window.

Six people steamed off Paul's porch and came roaring across the driveway.

"Gibson! Hey! Hey!" the bus driver was shouting.

Mr. Gibson skipped to the front door nimbly, limp and all. He was terribly, amazingly, glad to see them. Life throbbed in the house suddenly when in trooped Lee Coffey with Virginia on the end of his arm. Then Theo Marsh—flippety-flop—his seamed face beaming, and young Jeanie, ducking lithely under his waving limbs. And then Paul, holding the door for the looming up of Mrs. Boatright, who came in like an ocean liner.

"*We found it!*" they all shouted.

"Everything's under control," yelped Lee, who was waving a sheet of paper. "The marines have landed! We did it, after all!" He pounded Mr. Gibson on the back rather violently. "*No* sting! O grave, where is thy . . . !" he babbled.

"*Tell us*," screamed Rosemary, over the noise, "*one* of you—"

"This Jeanie child," roared Theo Marsh, "this Jeanie is so sound and intelligent that *I* am lying in the dust at her feet. Fool! Fool, that I am! My life! My work!" He snatched the paper from the bus driver.

"But what—?"

The nurse said, "Well, *tell* them!" Then *she* told them. "It was Jeanie who asked Theo to *draw* the face he'd seen."

"And he drew it *so well*," cried Jeanie aglow, "that Grandma recognized her!"

The paper was thrust under Mr. Gibson's nose. A few pencil lines—a face, a beauty.

"Mama said it was Mrs. Violette," yelled Paul, "and I couldn't believe her. *I* never thought she was so darned lovely."

"Have eyes . . . and see not," droned the artist. His hair stood on end. He held the drawing in both hands and moved it softly to and fro. "Has she ever done any modeling?" he crooned. "These exquisite nostrils!"

"But what—" gasped Mr. Gibson, "what's *happened!*"

"Virginia called up her house," explained Lee excitedly. "This Violette or whatever. And it *was* this Violette. Some sister or other was there and this sister says, Yes, she *had* it!"

"This sister ha—?"

"Mrs. Violette *had* it!" boomed Paul. "She's gone to the mountains. She took it with her! But Mrs. Boatright called the police . . ."

Lee said, "And *she's* buddies with the high brass. *She* told *them* what to do, all right." He spanked Mrs. Boatright on the shoulders. "Hey, Mary Anne?"

"They will stop her car," said Mrs. Boatright calmly, "or truck, as I believe it is. We secured the license number. An all-points-bulletin. The organization is quite capable." Mrs. Boatright was beaming like Santa Claus, for all her calm.

"So you *see!*" gasped Virginia. "She's not going to use it en route. How *could* she? So you are saved!"

Ethel stood there.

"Furthermore," said Mrs. Boatright, looking around as

if this were a committee, "I see no reason, at all, since
there has been no catastrophe, for *any* further proceeding.
Justice will not be served by publicity or by punishment.
Mr. Gibson is not going to kill himself. Nor will he ever
do such a thing as he did. I do believe that I convinced
Chief Miller . . . If not, I will."

"You did already," cried Lee. "You beat it into him,
Mary Anne. Believe me, you were superb! So All's Well
that Ends Well! Hey? Hey?"

"Hey?" joined Theo.

Rosemary made a little whimpering sound of relief and
staggered and drooped into a chair.

"Is there any brandy?" said the nurse anxiously, ob-
serving this collapse with a professional eye.

Ethel stood there. She had no idea what was happening. She understood nothing. "Brandy in the kitchen," she
said mechanically, "left-hand cupboard, over the sink
. . ." Her face went into a kind of social simper. She expected to be introduced to them all.

But the nurse ran toward the kitchen with the bus
driver on the end of her arm.

The telephone rang and Mrs. Boatright rolled in her
swift smooth way to answer it.

It was Theo Marsh who turned, elbows out, chin forward, eyes malicious, and said loudly, "So this is Ethel?
Lethal Ethel?"

"Really," said Ethel, turning a dull red, "who *are* these
people!"

Mr. Gibson, trembling in every limb, had fallen into a
chair himself. He realized that Ethel was completely at
a loss. She was not on the same level as the rest of them.
She couldn't understand their swift communications. She'd
been insulted besides . . . But he could not speak, for he
was saved who had been doomed, and he tingled and was
dumb.

Rosemary said weakly, "We were just going to tell
you—just a min—" She gasped to silence.

There was a silence as they all understood this with
surprise. Ethel did not *know?*

Mrs. Boatright spoke into the phone, "Yes, he is
here. . . . But may I take a message—? The Laboraory?
Oh, I see. But it *has* been found, you know, and no harm
done at all. . . . Oh, you did? . . . No, you couldn't have
known at that time. . . . I see. . . . Oh no, it was never

loose upon the public. That was just an error. . . ." She
went on murmuring.

Out in the kitchen the nurse found the brandy with
dispatch, but then Lee, with enterprise, embraced her.
They stood in a clinch. A green paper bag lay on top of
the other trash in the kitchen wastebasket. The bottle,
with King Roberto's picture on it, stood upside down
on the counter. But they whispered, and they were not
looking at the scenery.

In the living room, Theo bared his particolored teeth
at Ethel. (Mrs. Boatright was too busy on the phone to
restrain him, for now she was calling to have a car sent.)
So Theo said, "Ethel herself? The dead-end kid? The
doom preacher? The amateur psychiatrist?"

Ethel looked as if she would choke.

"I cannot see," she cried, hoarse with rage, "why a perfect freak of a strange old man is permitted to come in
here and call me names! Until somebody in this room
makes sense, I intend to eat my dinner, which—" her
voice rose to a scream—"*is getting cold!*"

Ethel never could bear an interruption in her schedule,
or any surprises. She went to the table and sat down with
a plop and plunged her fork blindly into the congealing
mass of the spaghetti. Theo Marsh drifted after her. He
leaned on the wall and watched—his head cocked.

But to Mr. Gibson, in the chair, in the living room, his
senses were returning. His eyes were clearing. He had
assimilated the news, the wonderful surprise. He was
saved. He was free. He loved and was loved and nobody
was going to die of the poison, and prayers are really
answered for all a human being dares to *know,* and he
looked about with relish to receive the sense of home—
his dear—his earthly home.

And his breath stopped.

"Rosemary! he cried. "What is *that?* On the mantel?"

"What, darling?" Rosemary, who had risen, restless
with joy, moved, drunken with relief. "This?" She took
a ball of mustard-colored string up in her hand. "There's
money here," she said wonderingly, "where the blue vase
used to stand."

So Mr. Gibson, his wits working as fast as ever they
had in his life, quickened with terror, plunged like a
quarterback between Paul and Jeanie past the body of

Theo Marsh to seize the loaded fork from the hand of his sister, Ethel.

"Mrs. Violette was *here!*" he shouted.

"Really, Ken, I couldn't say," said Ethel huffily. "But you left every door in this house unlocked and we could have been robbed . . ." She was livid with anger.

"Olive oil!" he shouted. "A bottle of olive oil! *Where is it?*"

"In the sauce," said Ethel. "I presumed you meant it for the sauce." Her brows were at the top of their possible ascent. "Have you gone mad?" she inquired frigidly.

At this moment the nurse and the bus driver came on loud quick feet. "What's *this!*" Virginia said. She had a glass of brandy in one hand and a small empty glass bottle in the other, which bottle she shook at them.

"And this! *Hey!*" puffed Lee Coffey, showing them the green paper bag.

"It's *here,*" said Mr. Gibson. "Don't touch it, Ethel! It is a deadly poison!"

"Poison?" she said recoiling.

Mr. Gibson scraped spaghetti off all three plates into the bowl and then he took up the bowl in a grim clutch. "It must have been Mrs. Violette who spoke to me," he told them. "She did have to go to the bank. I remember she said so. She took the bus, down and back. She spoke the second time when she *saw* me leave it in the seat. *She knew it was mine.* She brought it back with the string!"

"She is so very honest . . ." said Rosemary awesomely.

"That's *it?*" cried Theo. "You *got* the poison, *there?*"

"It's here. And it's been here all afternoon," said Mr. Gibson, and he took the bowl tenderly with him and sat down and held it on his lap and bowed his head.

"We must inform the police," said Mrs. Boatright briskly—but with deep pleasure.

"We are all heroes," said the bus driver.

But Jeanie Townsend, girl heroine, stood with all the other heroes, and frowned. "But why doesn't Miss Gibson *know* about the poisoned olive oil?" she asked. "I heard them telling all about it . . . on *her* radio. *This* one, right here."

"I . . . don't under—what poison?" said Ethel, rising, tottering. "I don't understand. Olive oil?"

Paul began, "He stole it from my lab . . ."

"The laboratory called earlier," said Mrs. Boatright

sharply. "They were just on the line. They had discovered their loss. The police had not got to them then. But surely, they *must* have told you about your brother who had the *only* opportunity—"

"I—took a message," said Ethel thickly. "Nobody mentioned . . . poison? Did Ken have poison?" Her eyes rolled.

"He was going to do himself in," said the bus driver chattily. "But he thinks better of it now."

"Do himself . . . *what?* Please . . ."

"He thinks better of it now," said Rosemary shakily. "Oh, darling, have we really found it?"

"Right here," said Mr. Gibson. "I've *got* it." He tightened his tight fingers. Rosemary looked angelic, suddenly, as if she would now fly up to the ceiling on great white wings.

"Je-ust a minute," said Theo Marsh. He looked at Lee Coffey. "What have we here?" he inquired. "Hoist?"

"Hoist! Hoist!" croaked the bus driver. "I see what you mean. With her own petard." He flung out one arm.

"Uh-*huh*," said Theo. "We better analyze this. Now, Ethel . . ." He rounded upon her. "You know, of course, that we are all impelled by subconscious forces. Primitive and low. Hey?" (He had picked up the bus driver's "hey.")

Ethel looked absolutely stupid.

"You say you didn't 'hear' the warning? Hah-hah-hah." The artist gave forth a mirthless sound. "But the subconscious hears all things, my dear. Now, *you* know that. Then the laboratory phoned. But told you *nothing?* Nor did you ask?"

"Likely story, all right," said Lee cheerfully. "Where was *your* subconscious . . . hey? All God's chillun got sub—"

"Her subconscious was putting two and two together," said Theo, shouting him down. "Therefore it is *obvious,* is it not, Ethel? *You wished to kill your brother and his wife. You must have.*"

Ethel stared at him.

"Because you nearly *did* kill them, you know," said Theo. "There *is* a deadly poison in that sauce. Don't try to tell us you never 'meant' to do it." He put his thumbs in the armholes of his vest. He looked like the sheriff in a Western.

"I . . ." croaked Ethel, "I had no warning . . . I don't

understand. . . . Please." Her wits seemed to return. "You mean we would have become ill?"

"You would have become dead," said the bus driver.

Her eyes popped, staring.

"Failing this," said Theo, "you then obviously *wished to kill yourself.*" Theo veered to the bus driver. "Say, how does that come in?"

"We'll figure something," said the driver enthusiastically. "*We'll* tell her what her motive was."

"Sex?" said Theo, brightening.

Mr. Gibson was speechless.

Rosemary said indignantly, "It *doesn't* come in. *Stop it,* both of you."

"Subconsciously," began the artist, his bright malicious glance examining his victim.

"Theo," said Mrs. Boatright.

"Lee," said Virginia in exactly the same tone. The bus driver's shoulders dropped, his arms turned outward in a gesture of apology and relaxation. But he was grinning.

Mr. Gibson, however, watched his wife. Adoringly. (My darling, he thought, is truly kind and compassionate of heart. And if this is innocent, how sweet it is, this innocence, how lovely!) For Rosemary stood beside Ethel, furiously defending her.

"Ethel just does not *hear words* when she turns on music. She has *trained* herself *not* to. She really *wouldn't* have heard the warning. She is *not* trying to kill anybody. She *didn't* mean to. She *couldn't* have. It would have been an *accident*. And *you know it,*" she defied the artist, "and don't be so *mean,* now."

"Rosemary," said Ethel brokenly, reaching for her. "I don't understand this . . . honestly. I certainly wouldn't want to hurt you or anyone . . . honestly—"

"Of course not," said Rosemary, caressing her as one would comfort a frightened child. "Don't you pay any attention to these cut-ups. Now, I believe you'd never mean to, Ethel."

Mr. Gibson thought dizzily, Rosemary and I must try to help poor Ethel . . . poor, brave, unlucky Ethel, faithless, cheated of love. He seemed to himself to pass out for a moment or two. Everybody seemed to be telling Ethel the whole sequence, and he could not bear it. He revived to find himself still sitting in the chair with the bowl of poisoned food tight in his hands. He looked about him.

Now Ethel sat alone.

Mrs. Walter Boatright was on the phone telling the police department exactly what it was to do now. (It would do as she said. He had no doubt.)

The little nurse, finding nobody interested in the brandy, had slipped to the floor beside Ethel's chair and sat there thoughtfully sipping it herself.

The bus driver and the painter were wringing each other by the hand, the artist literally hopping up and down in intellectual delight and still muttering, "Hoist! Hoist!"

"Judge not! Hey?" said the bus driver. "The biter bit. A bitter bite."

Jeanie had run for the door in a streak, a moment ago (now he recalled), yelling, "I'll tell Grandma." And Paul, who had been hugging her, in his joy, now hugged Rosemary. (Anybody. Any soft huggable body. Mr. Gibson understood perfectly.)

He hugged the bowl and thought, Now who could predict such a scene as this? He felt delighted.

But he did not contemplate it long. Hanging onto the bowl, he plunged into the celebration, himself, in person.

A police car had slipped into the drive; now a cop got out.

He was young, and not too sure what he'd been sent here for. He approached the door of the cottage. Before he could ring, it was swinging in before him with a tremendous welcoming verve, pulled by a small, compact man with dancing eyes. This man had a slight, brown-haired, merry-eyed woman tucked under his other arm. She was smiling too, and she helped balance, between them, what looked to be a wooden bowl full of spaghetti. These two stepped back in unison, like a pair of dancers, bowing him inward.

In the small foyer, a big handsome gent was crooning into the telephone. "It's O.K., dear. It really *is!* Everything is wonderful and I'll be home soon." (The cop had no way of knowing he was talking to his mother-in-law.)

In the living room, a wiry old gentleman in a pink shirt whistling tunelessly through his teeth, and with his thin legs prancing, was enthusiastically steering the majestic bulk of a beige-and-white-clad matron in the waltz. She stepped lightly.

Another man, in a leather jacket, crouched for the purpose of kissing the not unwilling lips of a cool little Nordic blonde who was sitting on the floor. From a tiny glass in her limp hand, something trickled on the back of his neck. He wasn't minding.

The cop's eye assessed all this. He was here, he supposed, to ask questions. "I dunno much about this," he confessed, looking at the plain-faced, middle-aged woman who sat in the midst of all the hilarity, stricken and still, staring at the carpet (as if she'd been shook, all right, he thought). "Is she the one," he said aside with pity, "who got careless with some poison?"

The man at the door hesitated. Then he said, "No, it was I. But mercifully . . . Come in. Come in," said Mr. Gibson cordially. *"I'm all right now."*